As he bent his dark head and kissed her mouth her eyes closed helplessly, shutting out the world and leaving only sensation.

Just at first his lips felt cold. Then the coldness turned to heat as his mouth moved lightly against hers, making every nerve ending in her body sing into life and sending her head spinning.

Though Jenny had been kissed many times, and though most of those kisses had been long and ardent, somehow they had failed to move her, leaving her feeling untouched, aloof, uninvolved.

But while Michael's thistledown kiss couldn't have lasted more than a few seconds, by the time he lifted his head her legs would no longer hold her, and her very soul seemed to have lost its way....

LEE WILKINSON attended an all girls school, where her teachers, often finding her daydreaming, declared that she "lived inside her own head," and that is still largely true today. Until her marriage she had a variety of jobs, ranging from PA to a departmental manager, to modeling swimsuits and underwear.

An only child and avid reader from an early age, she began writing when she, her husband and their two children moved to Derbyshire, U.K. She started with short stories and magazine serials before going on to write romances for Harlequin®.

A lover of animals, Lee adopted a rescue dog named Thorn, after losing Kelly, her adored German shepherd. Thorn looks like a pit bull and acts like a big softy, apart from when the postman calls. Then he has to be restrained, otherwise he goes berserk and shreds the mail.

Traveling has always been one of Lee's main pleasures, and after crossing Australia and America in a motor home, and traveling round the world on two separate occasions she still, periodically, suffers from itchy feet.

She enjoys walking and cooking, log fires and red wine, music and the theater, and still much prefers books to television—both reading and writing them.

CAPTIVE IN THE MILLIONAIRE'S CASTLE

LEE WILKINSON

~ DARK NIGHTS WITH A BILLIONAIRE ~

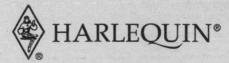

TORONTO • NEW YORK • LONDON
AMSTERDAM • PARIS • SYDNEY • HAMBURG
STOCKHOLM • ATHENS • TOKYO • MILAN • MADRID
PRAGUE • WARSAW • BUDAPEST • AUCKLAND

Recycling programs
for this product may
not exist in your area.

ISBN-13: 978-0-373-52740-3

CAPTIVE IN THE MILLIONAIRE'S CASTLE

First North American Publication 2009.

Copyright © 2009 by Lee Wilkinson.

CAPTIVE IN THE
MILLIONAIRE'S CASTLE

CHAPTER ONE

FEBRUARY the fourteenth.

The headlines in the morning paper read:

A WELL-DESERVED VALENTINE FOR WELL-KNOWN AUTHOR. For the second year running, Michael Denver, who, according to some of the top literary critics, is unsurpassed in the field of psychological thrillers, has won the prestigious Quentin Penman Literary Award, this time for his new book, *Withershins*. This makes him one of the most celebrated authors of his day, with five award-winning novels to his credit.

In spite of this, Michael Denver, after hitting the headlines with a high-profile divorce from top model Claire Falconer, and subsequent rumours of a reconciliation, guards his privacy fiercely and refuses to be either interviewed or photographed.

His four previous books have been snapped up by Hollywood and three of them have already become major box-office successes. Having been widely acclaimed, and quoted as being 'his best so far,' *Withershins* seems likely to follow suit.

Michael replaced the receiver and ran his fingers through his thick dark hair. The phone call from his long-time friend, Paul Levens, had finally served to make up his mind.

Well, almost.

He could do with a PA, and if Paul was right and this girl was the treasure he claimed she was, she might be just what he wanted.

No, not wanted. *Needed.*

For quite a while, hating the idea of working with another person rather than on his own, as he was used to, Michael had put off the evil moment. But now, of necessity, he was having to think again.

When Paul, who had just reached the position of Associate Director at Global Enterprises, had casually mentioned that he knew of the ideal woman to fill the position, Michael had raised various objections, all of which—unusually for him— were anything but logical.

'Look,' Paul said, his blue eyes serious, 'I'm well aware that after the way women threw themselves at you following your divorce the entire female sex are anathema to you, but it isn't like you to let emotions, especially such destructive ones, overrule your common sense.

'You *need* a good PA. And I'm offering you the chance of a really first-class one. Believe me, Jennifer Mansell is as good as you're going to get.'

With devastating logic, Michael demanded, 'If she's that good, why are you letting her go?'

'Because I have little option. The powers that be have decided that in the present economic climate we *have* to trim staff wherever possible.

'Arthur Jenkins, the departmental boss she's worked for for more than three years, recently suffered a heart attack and is retiring on doctors' orders.'

As Michael was about to interrupt he hurried on, 'If it had

been simply a matter of replacing Jenkins, that would have more or less kept the status quo. But it isn't.

'Home Sales are being amalgamated with Export, and Cutcliff, who's run Export for over ten years, already has a good PA.'

A gleam of amusement in his forest-green eyes, Michael suggested dryly, 'So you're trying to palm this Jennifer Mansell off on me?'

Paul, a fair-haired, beefy rugby forward, sighed. 'I'm trying to help you. Though God alone knows why.'

Michael grunted. 'Well, I'll think about it.'

Raising his eyes to heaven, Paul said with some exasperation, 'Don't overdo the gratitude, whatever you do.'

Grinning, Michael clapped his friend on the shoulder. 'Thanks.'

But, for him, agreeing to have a woman in his office, under his feet, was a drastic step.

Perhaps if Paul's protégée had been a man... But even then, he wasn't sure if he could tolerate the presence of anyone else.

After almost a week, though he really needed to be at his rural retreat, Slinterwood, and starting on his latest book, he had still been undecided.

Then he had received a phone call from his ex-wife, Claire, telling him how badly she missed him and how much she wanted him back in her life, which had done nothing to improve his mood.

Her apparent conviction that she just had to snap her fingers to get him back had made him bitterly angry, and only served to reinforce his present dislike of women. Especially the ones who used sex as a weapon, as she had.

That same morning, Paul had rung and informed him flatly, 'Well, this is your last chance. On Friday evening Miss Mansell will be hostess at Jenkins's retirement party. After that, she'll be leaving.'

Getting no immediate response, he suggested, 'Tell you what, why don't you take a quick look at her, see what you think? She's easy on the eye without being too distracting. And I'm quite sure that she's not the kind to throw herself at you.

'If you want to actually meet her, I can introduce you simply as a friend of mine. If not, you can stay in the background, do the whole thing discreetly.'

In no mood for a party, Michael chose the latter course.

'In the meantime,' Paul promised, 'I'll find out as much as I can about her.'

At eight o'clock that Friday evening, partly concealed by the luxurious foliage of one of the decorative plants, Michael was standing on the balcony that encircled the Mayfair Hotel's sumptuous ballroom, where Arthur Jenkins's retirement party was taking place.

Already he was half regretting coming. Admittedly he needed a good PA, but a good PA didn't *have* to be a woman. Still, to pacify Paul, he would stay long enough to hear what he had to say, and take a look at this Miss Mansell.

From the vantage point he had chosen almost opposite the raised dais, where later a presentation was to be made, he was able to get a commanding view over the assembled company.

An orchestra at present occupying the dais was playing dance music, and quite a lot of couples were circling the floor, while the remainder of the guests were standing in groups laughing and talking as the waiters dispensed champagne.

It was a truly glittering occasion. Arthur Jenkins had been with Global Enterprises for over thirty years, so in spite of the threatened economical slow-down no expense had been spared.

The woman Michael had come specifically to see wasn't in evidence. So far he'd only glimpsed her from a distance. Tall and slim with dark hair taken up in an elegant swirl, she was wearing an ankle-length chiffon dress in muted, south-sea-colour shades of aquamarine, lapis lazuli and gold.

Paul, the only other person who knew he was there, had pointed her and Arthur Jenkins out to him.

'What did you manage to find out about her?' Michael asked quietly.

'Not a great deal,' Paul answered. 'The only information Personnel could give me was that she's twenty-four years old, quiet, efficient, and came to Global straight from a London business college.

'The people she worked with say she did her job well, and described her as having a friendly manner, but tending to keep herself to herself.'

'Anything else?'

'Very little's known about her private life but I did manage to pick up, from the grapevine, that for some time she wore an engagement ring.

'After she stopped wearing it, a few months ago, it appears that several of the men in the office tried their luck, but all of them were given a very cool reception, not to say the cold shoulder. It seems she's gone off men.'

Michael frowned thoughtfully. From that brief report, Jennifer Mansell sounded ideal.

However, reluctant to admit as much, he merely said, 'Thanks for the information.'

Paul shrugged heavy shoulders. 'Such as it is. Well, I'd better go and circulate. I take it you don't want to meet her now?'

Shaking his head, Michael answered, 'No.'

'Well, when you've managed to get a good look at her, if you do change your mind, just let me know.' Paul sketched a brief salute before heading for the stairs.

Michael was waiting only a minute or so when Arthur Jenkins and Jennifer Mansell came into view once again.

With no unseemly display of thigh or bosom, the simply

cut dress she was wearing showed off her slender, graceful figure to perfection.

As she got closer he noticed that on her right wrist she was wearing a small watch on a plain black strap, and, on her right hand, a gold ring.

Her dark head was turned away from him as she conversed with her portly companion.

For some strange reason—a kind of premonition, perhaps— Michael found himself oddly impatient to see her face.

When she did turn towards him she was smiling, and he caught his breath. He *knew* that face, and not just because something about her reminded him of a young Julia Roberts.

Though they had never actually met, he had seen her before. But where and when?

And then he remembered, and he found his heart beating faster as he relived the little scene that had taken place at the castle, was it five years ago or six?

It had been late afternoon and, the only visitor still remaining, she had been standing in the cobbled courtyard, bright with its tubs of flowers.

Head tilted back, a coolish breeze ruffling her long dark hair, she had been watching some early swallows wheeling overhead, smiling then, as she was smiling now. He had been standing on the battlements, looking down. Still smiling, she had glanced in his direction. For a long moment their eyes had met and held, until, as though shy, she had looked away.

Though he hadn't had the faintest idea why, even then she had seemed familiar to him, as if he had always known her.

Seeing her start to head towards the main gate, he had turned to hurry after her. But by the time he had descended the spiral stone stairway of the north tower she had vanished from sight.

Impelled by a sudden urgency, he had moved swiftly across the courtyard and beneath the portcullis. At the bottom of the steep, cobbled path that led up to the castle gate, a car had been just pulling away.

He had tried to attract her attention, to no avail. As he had stood there the car had bumped down the uneven dirt road, turned right, and disappeared round the curve of the rocky hill.

Climbing up to the battlements again, with a strange sense of loss he had watched the silver dot take the picturesque coastal road that skirted the island, and head in the direction of the causeway.

To all intents and purposes the little incident was over, finished, but he had thought about her, wondered about her, and her face had stayed etched indelibly in his memory.

He had tried to play his disappointment down, to tell himself that he couldn't possibly feel so strongly about a woman he had only glimpsed, and never actually met. But wherever he went he had found himself scanning the faces of people passing by, unconsciously looking for her.

Over time, the impact she had had on him had gradually faded into the recesses of his mind, but he had never totally forgotten.

Now here she was again, as though fate had decreed it, and he was strangely shaken to see her once more.

In spite of his present aversion to women, he was tempted to go down, to see her at close quarters, to speak to her and hear her voice.

But common sense held him back.

Everything had changed. Instead of being a twenty-two year old with romantic ideals, he was older and wiser, not to say battle-scarred and bitter, with a newly acquired mistrust of women. And though her face was poignantly familiar, he didn't know what kind of woman she really was.

As he stood watching a tall, balding man detached her from Arthur Jenkins's side and led her onto the dance floor, where they were immediately swallowed up in the crowd.

Michael ran thoughtful fingers over his smooth chin. His inclination was to get to know her better, but, with all his previous reservations still intact, he didn't feel inclined to rush things…

He was standing staring blindly over the throng of dancers when Paul reappeared and remarked, 'So you're still here? I wasn't sure how long you intended to stay.'

'I was planning to leave shortly,' Michael told him, 'but I wanted another word with you first.'

'You've had a look at her, I take it? So what do you think?'

'From what I've seen so far, your recommendation appears to have been a good one, but—'

An expression of resignation on his face, Paul broke in, 'But you're not going to do anything about it! Oh, well, it's up to you, of course. But I personally believe it would be a mistake to let her slip through your fingers without at least taking things a step further.'

'I have every intention of taking things a step further,' Michael said quietly. 'But as this is neither the time nor the place, I'd like you to have a quick word with her and tell her…'

A group of chattering, laughing people paused nearby, and he lowered his voice even more to finish what he was saying.

'Will do,' Paul promised crisply as Michael clapped him on the shoulder before striding away.

Hearing a car turn into the quiet square lined with skeletal trees, Laura went to the window and peeped through a chink in the curtains.

She was just in time to see a taxi draw up in front of the block of flats, and Jenny climb out and cross the frosty pavement.

'Hi,' Laura greeted her flatmate laconically as she came into the living-room.

'Hi.' Tossing aside her evening wrap, and glancing at Laura's pink fluffy dressing gown and feathery mules, Jenny observed, 'I thought you'd be tucked up in bed by now.'

Her round, baby-face shiny with night cream, and the long blonde hair that earlier in the evening she had spent ages straightening once again starting to curl rebelliously, Laura agreed. 'I would have been, but Tom and I went out to Whistlers, and we had to wait ages for a taxi back.

'How did the party go?'

'Very well,' Jenny answered sedately.

Noting her flatmate's sparkling eyes and her barely concealed air of excitement, Laura asked, 'What is it? Did Prince Charming turn up and sweep you off your feet?'

'No, nothing like that.'

'So what's happened to make you look like the fifth of November? Come on, do tell.'

'I could do with a cup of tea first,' Jenny suggested hopefully.

'You drive a hard bargain,' Laura complained as she disappeared kitchenwards. 'But as I could do with a cup myself…'

Slipping off her evening sandals, Jenny settled herself on the settee in front of the glowing gasfire, stretched her feet towards the warmth, and hugged the bubbling excitement to her.

After starting the evening in low spirits, knowing that she no longer had a job, Jenny was now on top of the world, with the hope of new things opening up.

She hadn't felt so happy since Andy's perfidy had torn her world apart, making her feel betrayed and unwanted, worthless even.

Laura returned quite quickly carrying two steaming mugs. Handing one to Jenny, she plonked herself down and urged, 'Right. Spill it.'

'You know Michael Denver?'

'You mean the writer? The one you've always been nuts about?'

'I wouldn't put it quite like that.'

'Why not? It's the truth…'

And it was. Since reading his first book, Jenny had been hooked, fascinated, not only by his intricate mind games and clever, complex plots, but by the brain behind them.

Yet for all their brilliance his books were easy to read, and his writing had compassion and sensitivity. His characters were real people with faults and failings and weaknesses, but also with courage and spirit and strength. People that his readers could understand and care about.

'So what about Michael Denver?' Laura pursued.

'He's in need of a PA, and I'm being interviewed for the job.'

Laura's jaw dropped. 'You don't mean interviewed by the man himself?'

Jenny nodded. 'Apparently.'

'When?'

'Eight-thirty tomorrow morning.'

'It's Saturday tomorrow,' Laura pointed out.

'Yes, I know. But it seems he's in a hurry to fill the post. He's sending a car for me. I can hardly believe it.'

'Neither can I. Are you quite sure you haven't had too much champagne?'

'Positive.'

'So how come?'

'It appears that Mr Jenkins, bless him, has sung my praises to Paul Levens, one of Global's directors, who happens to be a friend of Michael Denver's.

'When there was no available job for me with Global, Mr Levens, who knew that Michael Denver needed a PA, suggested me.'

'And bingo!'

'It may not be that simple. I may not get the job. But I certainly hope I do. It would be a dream come true to work for someone like him.'

Laura grunted. 'Well, all I can say is, if he doesn't realize how lucky he is and snap you up, he's an idiot.'

Smiling at her friend's aggressive loyalty, Jenny said, 'Well, we'll just have to wait and see.'

Finishing her tea, she added, 'Now I'd better get off to bed, so I have my wits about me for the interview. I get the feeling that Michael Denver isn't one to suffer fools gladly.'

Pulling a disappointed face, Laura protested, 'Spoilsport. I was just going to ask you what you've found out about him.'

'Hardly anything. But I'll tell you what little I do know in the morning.'

'It's a deal! Sleep well.'

The following morning, after a restless night, Jenny was up early. By the time she had finished showering, her flatmate, who usually slept late on a Saturday, was already pottering round the kitchen making toast and coffee.

'Sheer nosiness,' she confessed in answer to Jenny's query. 'I couldn't wait to hear all about the man himself. And I wanted to be up just in case he came in person to collect you.'

'It's hardly likely,' Jenny said dryly.

'Well, at least I'll get to see his car... Now then, what about some toast?'

Shaking her head, Jenny admitted, 'I'm too nervous to eat a thing. But I will have a coffee.'

Laura poured two cups before asking with unrestrained eagerness, 'So what did you find out about him?'

'Very little, except that he lives in a quiet block of flats in Mayfair.' In a portentous voice, she added, 'These days everything about him is shrouded in mystery.'

Only half believing her, Laura asked, 'Honestly?'

'Honestly.'

'Why? There must be a reason.'

'Well, as most of it seems to be public knowledge already, I'll tell you what Mr Levens told me.

'When Michael Denver first shot to fame after winning his second award, he became an overnight celebrity. But it seems that he's a man who values his privacy, and he did his utmost to play it down and stay in the background.

'Then he met and married a top photographic model named Claire Falconer—'

'Oh, yes, I know her!' Laura exclaimed. 'Or rather I know *of* her.' Then impatiently, 'Go on.'

'Both "beautiful people" and celebrities, they seemed to be madly in love with each other and ideally suited.

'The media soon nicknamed them the Golden Couple, and followed them everywhere with their cameras. But while *she* enjoyed all the fuss and the media attention, *he* loathed it.

'The attention was just starting to die down when a story that she'd been seen in the bedroom of a secluded hotel with another man while her husband was away got into the papers. She claimed it was a lie. But a follow-up story included a photograph of the pair of them trying to slip out of the hotel the next morning.

'That gave rise to rumours that after only six months the marriage was breaking up, and the press had a field day. Michael Denver stayed tight-lipped and refused to comment, but his wife gave an interview in which she announced that she still loved him and was trying for a reconciliation. What he'd hoped would be a quiet divorce degenerated into a three-ringed circus—'

'Now you mention it, I do remember reading about it. At the time I felt rather sorry for him.'

'I gather from what Mr Levens told me that between his ex-wife, who continued to oppose the divorce, and the attentions of the gutter press, his life was made almost intolerable.

'His refusal to give interviews or be photographed just made the paparazzi keener, and in the end he was forced to move flats and go to ground.'

'It must have been tough for the poor devil.'

'I'm sure it was.'

'Do you know, in spite of all that press coverage I've no idea how old he is or what he looks like, have you?'

'Not the faintest,' Jenny admitted.

'My guess is that he'll be middle-aged, handsome in a lean and hungry way, with a domed forehead, a beaky nose and a pair of piercing blue eyes.'

'What about his ears?'

'Oh, a pair of those too. Unless he's a tortured genius like Vincent Van Gogh.'

'Fool! I meant flat or sticky out?'

'Definitely sticky out, large, and a bit pointed.'

'What makes you think that?'

'Because that's what a brilliant writer *ought* to look like.' Jenny laughed. 'Well, if you say so.'

'By the way, if you get back to find the flat empty, don't be surprised. It's Tom's parents' wedding anniversary, and later we're off to Kent to spend the day with them.'

'Well, I hope everything goes really well. Do give Mr and Mrs Harmen my best wishes.'

Her coffee finished, Jenny dressed in a taupe suit and toning blouse, swept her hair into a smooth coil, added neat gold studs to her ears and the merest touch of make-up.

With just a mental picture of Michael Denver, and no real idea of his age or what he might want in a PA, she could only hope he would approve of her businesslike appearance.

The car, a chauffeur-driven Mercedes, drew up outside dead on time.

Laura, who was stationed by the window, exclaimed excitedly, 'It's here! Well, off you go, and the best of luck.'

Trying to quell the butterflies that danced in her stomach, Jenny picked up her shoulder bag, and said, 'Thanks. Enjoy your day.'

Outside, the air was cold, and Jack Frost had sprinkled the pavement with diamond dust and scrawled his glittering autograph over natural and man-made objects alike.

By the kerb, the elderly chauffeur was standing smartly to attention, waiting to open the car door for her.

As she reached him he bid a polite, 'Good morning, miss.'

Jenny returned the greeting and, feeling rather like some usurper masquerading as royalty, climbed in and settled herself into the warmth and comfort of the limousine.

By the time they reached Mayfair and drew up outside the sumptuous block of flats, she had managed to conquer the nervous excitement, and at least appear her usual cool, collected self.

Having crossed the marble-floored lobby, she identified herself to Security before taking the private lift up to the second floor, as instructed.

As the doors slid open and she emerged into a luxurious lobby she was met by a tall, thin butler with a long, lugubrious face. 'Miss Mansell? Mr Denver is expecting you. If you would like to follow me?'

She obeyed, and was ushered into a large, very well-equipped office.

'Miss Mansell, sir.'

As the door closed quietly behind her a tall, dark, broad-shouldered man dressed in smart casuals rose from his seat behind the desk.

A sudden shock ran through her, and though somehow her legs kept moving she felt as if she had walked slap bang into an invisible plate-glass window.

While she was convinced they had never met, she felt certain that she knew him. Some part of her *recognized* him, *remembered* him, *responded* to him…

But even as she tried to tell herself that she must, at one time, have seen his photograph in the papers, she felt quite certain that that wasn't the answer. Though there had to be some logical explanation for such a strong feeling.

Michael, for his part, was struggling to hide his relief. For a man who was normally so confident, so sure of himself and the plans he was putting into action, he had been unsettled and on edge. Half convinced that she wouldn't come, after all, and angry with himself that it *mattered*.

Now here she was, and though for some reason her steps had faltered and she had appeared to be momentarily disconcerted, she had quickly regained her composure.

Holding out his hand, he said without smiling, 'Miss Mansell... How do you do?'

His voice was low-pitched and attractive, his features clearcut, but tough and masculine rather than handsome.

'How do you do?' Putting her hand into his, and meeting those thickly lashed, forest-green eyes, sent tingles down her spine.

She had expected him to be middle-aged, but he was considerably younger, somewhere in his late twenties, she judged, and nothing at all like the picture Laura had painted of him.

At close quarters, Michael found, she was not merely beautiful, but intriguing. Her face held both character and charm, and a haunting poignancy that made him want to keep on looking at her.

Annoyed by his own reaction, he said a shade brusquely, 'Won't you sit down?'

Despite the instant impact he had had on her, she found his curt manner more than a little off-putting, and she took the black leather chair he'd indicated, a shade reluctantly.

Resuming his own seat, he placed his elbows on the desk, rested his chin on his folded hands, and studied her intently.

Her small, heart-shaped face was calm and composed, her back straight, her long legs crossed neatly, her skirt drawn down demurely over her knees.

There was no sign of the femme fatale, not the faintest suggestion that she might try to employ any sexual wiles, which seemed to confirm that she was different from the women who had, in the wake of his divorce, seemed to think he was fair game.

Appreciating the natural look, after all the artificial glamour of the modelling world, he was pleased to note she wore very little make-up. But with a flawless skin and dark brows and lashes, she didn't need to.

Up close, the impact of those big brown eyes and the wide, passionate mouth was stunning. But though she was one of the loveliest and most fascinating women he had ever seen, it wasn't in a showy way.

Her hands were long and slender, strong hands in spite of their apparent delicacy, and he was pleased to see that her pale oval nails were buffed but mercifully unvarnished.

On her right hand he glimpsed the gold ring she had worn the previous night, but her left hand was bare.

Becoming aware that she was starting to look slightly uncomfortable under his silent scrutiny, and wanting to know more about her, he instructed briskly, 'Tell me about yourself.'

'What exactly would you like to know?'

She had a nice voice, he noted—always acutely sensitive to voices—soft and slightly husky.

'To start with, where you were born.'

'I was born in London.'

'And you've lived here all your life?'

'No. When I was quite small, we moved to the little town of Kelsay. It's on the east coast…'

With a little jolt of excitement, he said, 'Yes, I know it.' The fact that she came from Kelsay seemed to confirm— though he hadn't really *needed* any further confirmation—that she was the girl he had seen at the castle.

'So how come you're back in London?'

'When my great-grandmother, whom I was living with, died just a few weeks after I left school, I enrolled at the

London School of Business Studies. Then when I had the qualifications I needed, I applied for, and got, a job with Global Enterprises.

'I started work in the general office, then became PA to Mr Jenkins, one of the departmental heads.'

'I understand from Paul Levens that Mr Jenkins is retiring, and that the department he ran is being merged with another. Which is why you're looking for a new position?'

'That's right.'

'He also mentioned that Mr Jenkins spoke very highly of you, praising your loyalty, your tact and your efficiency. All attributes that as far as I'm concerned are essential.'

When she said nothing, merely looked at him steadily, he went on to ask, 'What, in your opinion, is a PA there for?'

'I've always thought that a good PA should keep things ticking over smoothly and do whatever it takes to keep her boss happy.'

'Even if it includes running his errands and making his coffee?'

'Yes,' she answered without hesitation.

Thinking that after some of the women he had known she was like a breath of fresh air, he asked, 'You wouldn't regard that as infra dig?'

'No.' Seriously, she added, 'I've always thought of a PA as a well-paid dogsbody.'

Managing to hide a smile, he said, 'Good. Though the majority of the work would involve taking shorthand then transferring it onto a word-processor, it's that part that slows me down, I'm looking for a PA who isn't going to quibble about exact duties.

'I also need someone who, as well as being efficient, is discreet and trustworthy.'

'Mr Levens explained that.'

'And you think you fit the bill?'

'Yes, I believe I do.'

'Though the monthly salary will stay the same, between books there may be longish periods when I won't need a PA at all.

'But I must warn you that when I *am* writing, I often work seven days a week, and should I decide to work in the evenings, I'll expect my PA to be available. Would you be happy with that kind of "all or nothing" arrangement?'

She answered, 'Yes,' without hesitation.

Michael was well satisfied with that firm 'yes'. If he did decide to give her the job, and it was still a big if, it sounded as if she might well take it.

CHAPTER TWO

JUST for a moment the thought stopped Michael in his tracks. Was he seriously considering letting a woman into his life again, even on a purely business basis?

He wished he could come up with a resounding *no way!* But somehow this woman was different. And he was strangely reluctant to let her walk away from him for a second time.

Glancing up, and finding Jenny was looking at him expectantly, he rounded up his straying thoughts and resumed his questioning. 'While you've been working for Global Enterprises, how many times have you been off sick?'

'None at all. Luckily, I'm very healthy.'

'Then we come to the question of salary, and holidays. The commencing salary would be...'

He named a sum so in excess of what she might have hoped for that she blinked.

'But I expect holidays to be fitted in during the slack periods. Any taken during the busy spells would need to be agreed on well in advance. Does that seem reasonable to you?'

'Perfectly reasonable,' she answered steadily.

Running lean fingers over his smooth jaw, he regarded her in a contemplative silence for a moment or two.

She was a very beautiful woman, and, even taking into

account a broken engagement, it was hard to believe that there was no current man in her life.

Deciding that that was one thing he ought to establish, he began carefully, 'Do you live alone?'

'I have a flatmate.'

'As distinct from a live-in lover?'

A little stiffly, she objected, 'I'm afraid I don't see why my private life is relevant.'

His face cold, he said, 'It's relevant on more than one count. Apart from the long hours which this kind of work sometimes involves, when I begin a new book I prefer to leave London and work in comparative isolation, where I can be quite free from any unwanted social distractions.'

'Oh…'

Deciding to spell it out, he added, 'Which means I need a PA who is free from any personal commitments or obligations.'

'I see,' she said slowly.

'Is that a problem for you?'

She shook her head. 'No, not really.'

No nearer to finding out what he wanted to know, he applied a little more pressure.

'Then you have no ties? For example, no fiancé, who would almost certainly object?'

'No.'

Well, that seemed decided enough. Though he knew to his cost that, if it suited them, some women could lie with composure.

'And you don't dislike the thought of having to leave London?'

'No, not at all.'

She sounded as if she meant it.

He was oddly pleased.

Claire had hated the thought of leaving the bright lights of London and burying herself in what she referred to as 'the back of beyond', and after the first time she had refused point blank to go to Slinterwood again.

To please her, he had tried staying in town to finish writing *Mandrake,* but after several unproductive weeks he had given it up as hopeless.

With that important deadline fast approaching, she had suggested that he should go to Slinterwood while she remained in London.

Now, in retrospect, he could see that that had been the beginning of the end as far as their marriage was concerned…

Jenny was sitting quite still, but, sensing that she was once again growing uncomfortable with the lengthening silence, he went on, 'In that case I'm prepared to offer you a month's trial period.'

He hadn't *consciously* made up his mind, and his abrupt offer of a job had surprised even himself.

Jenny, also taken aback by the suddenness of the offer, hesitated, wishing she had more time to think.

Picking up the vibes, and sensing his earlier indecision, not to mention a certain amount of antagonism, she had expected further searching questions, and then a cool promise to 'let her know'.

She *wanted* the job, so she really ought to be over the moon, but she had found his attitude, and the intentness of his gaze, more than a little daunting

But that wasn't insurmountable, she told herself stoutly. The important thing was that she had been offered the chance to work for a writer she admired enormously, and even if her job was only to transcribe his words she wanted to be part of the creative process…

Now, watching her hesitate, and suddenly concerned that she was about to refuse after all, he asked brusquely, 'So what do you say?'

Telling herself that if it *did* prove to be a mistake, it was only for a month, she said, 'Thank you. I—I accept.'

He nodded. 'Good. Now the only thing is, how soon can you start?'

'Whenever you like.'

'Then let's say immediately.'

'You mean Monday?'

Deciding to strike while the iron was hot, he told her, 'I mean now.'

Sounding a little startled, she echoed, 'Now?'

'As I told you, when I begin a new book I prefer to leave London and work in comparative isolation. I was planning to go today. Seeing that you're free to start at once, it would be more convenient if you travelled with me.'

'Very well.'

'If my chauffeur takes you home, how long will you need to get organized and pack enough clothes for...shall we say...up to a month? Then we'll both be free to reassess the situation.'

'Half an hour at the most.'

'Excellent.

'By the time you get down to the lobby, the car will be outside, waiting. The car will drop you home and when you've had time to pack, I'll pick you up myself.'

'Thank you.'

Feeling as though she had been caught up and swept along by a tidal wave, she got to her feet and prepared to leave.

Wondering if he'd done the right thing, or if he'd allowed his subconscious feelings to hurry him into something he might regret, Michael rose to accompany her. If he found he *had* made a mistake he could always pay her for the month but get rid of her straight away.

Once again picking up the vibes, and not altogether at ease, Jenny headed for the door. Though at five feet seven inches she was tall for a woman, he was a good head taller, with a mature width of shoulder, and for once in her life she felt dwarfed, towered over.

As he opened the door the butler appeared as if by magic to escort her to the lift.

'I'll call for you in approximately an hour, depending on the traffic,' her new boss reminded her.

'I'll be ready,' she promised.

She had moved to join the manservant when a thought struck her, and, turning to Michael Denver, she began, 'Oh, by the way, where are we—?'

At the same instant the phone on his desk rang, and with a murmured, 'Excuse me,' he turned to answer it.

Oh, well, Jenny thought resignedly, she could find out exactly where they were going when he came to pick her up.

The Saturday morning traffic proved to be relatively light, and the drive back to her Bayswater flat was over quite quickly.

As good as her word, some half an hour after the chauffeur had dropped her Jenny's case was neatly packed with easy-care, mix-and-match stuff, and she was ready and waiting.

Smiling to herself, thinking of her flatmate's excitement when she read it, Jenny began to scrawl a hasty note.

Got the job, subject to a month's trial period. Will be starting immediately. Being whisked off to what I presume is his house in the country to begin work on his latest book.

Will be in touch. Jenny.

PS. The man himself is nothing like either of us pictured. He's quite young and not bad-looking, but rather cold and unapproachable, so he might not be pleasant to work for.

She had just finished writing when, glancing out of the window, she saw a large black four-wheel drive with tinted windows draw up by the kerb. It seemed somewhat out of place in London, but no doubt it would have its uses in the country.

Picking up her case and shoulder bag, her coat over her arm, she brushed aside the niggling doubt that she was doing the right thing, and hurried out.

The air was still cold, but the sun was now shining brightly from a clear, duck-egg-blue sky, and reflecting in the car's gleaming paintwork.

As she walked across the pavement Michael Denver opened the car door and jumped out, and she felt the same strange impact she'd felt on first seeing him.

'Good timing,' he congratulated her as he came round to take her case, before opening the car door.

By the time she had climbed in and fastened her seat belt he had stowed her case and was sliding behind the wheel once more.

While he skilfully threaded his way through the traffic, she stayed silent and tried to relax, but she was very conscious of him and could only manage, at the most, an *appearance* of tranquillity.

It wasn't until they had reached the suburbs and were heading out of London that she broached the question that had been at the back of her mind. 'By the way, Mr Denver—'

'I'd prefer to be on first-name terms,' he broke in coolly, 'if that's all right with you?'

She had expected him to retain the formality of surnames, at least for the time being, and, startled, she answered, 'Oh, yes… Quite all right…'

'Michael,' he prompted.

It seemed somehow momentous to be using his given name, and it took a second or two to pluck up enough courage to say, 'Michael.'

'And you're Jennifer?'

'Yes. But I usually get called Jenny.'

'Then Jenny it is. A nice old-fashioned name of Celtic origin,' he added. 'Now, you were about to ask me something?'

'Oh, yes… I still don't know where we're going. I presume you have a house somewhere in the country?'

'Yes, it's called Slinterwood.' His tone of voice holding an undercurrent of something she couldn't quite pin down, he added with apparent casualness, 'You know the Island of Mirren?'

'Of course.' Her voice held a little quiver of excitement. 'It's just down the coast from where my great-grandmother used to live.'

'Have you ever visited it?'

'I went once.'

'How long ago?'

'I was eighteen at the time. It was a short while before I moved to London.'

'You went to see Mirren Castle?'

'Yes. In those days it was open to the public at certain times.'

'What did you think of it?'

'I didn't see a great deal,' she admitted. 'I'd gone on the spur of the moment, quite late one afternoon, and I'd chosen the wrong day, which meant I couldn't go inside.

'But what I did see of the place was absolutely wonderful and I've never forgotten it. I had hoped to go back one day and see more of it.'

'And did you?' he pressed.

She shook her head. 'Things change, and by the time I had a chance it was too late. I heard that Mirren's new owner had closed the castle to the public and made it clear that visitors to the island were no longer welcome.'

'So you've never been back?'

'No.'

'Well, as you say, things change. But there's nothing to stop them changing again.'

She was wondering about that rather cryptic remark when he pursued, 'Did you ever find out who the new owner was?'

She shook her head. 'No. But I believe the island stayed in the hands of the same family. It was just a different policy in force.'

'A policy that caused you great disappointment?'

'Well, yes… Though I can't say I really blamed the new owner.'

In answer to her companion's questioning glance, she admitted, 'If it was mine, *I* wouldn't want visitors tramping around making a noise and dropping litter.'

When he said nothing, feeling the need to justify that remark, she added, 'I can't help but feel that a lot of the island's charm must lie in its isolation and the serenity that kind of isolation brings.'

Either her feelings echoed his own, or, he thought cynically, she was clever enough to realize that they were what his feelings *would* be, and to play up to him.

'Then you're not a gregarious creature?' he asked.

'No, not really.'

'Yet you chose to live in London.'

'I don't *dislike* London. It's an exciting, vibrant place to live, and of course it's where a lot of the jobs are.

'But after I'd left Kelsay I found I missed the sound of the sea and the dark night sky and the stars. With the glow from the street lamps it's not easy to see the stars in central London—' Suddenly realizing her tongue was running away with her, she broke off abruptly.

It wasn't at all like her to talk so freely to a man who was not only a virtual stranger but her new employer, and she wished she had been more circumspect, more restrained.

When he made no effort to break the ensuing silence, fearing she had already got off on the wrong foot, she apologized. 'I'm sorry, I'm afraid I was babbling. You can't possibly be interested in my—'

'Oh, but I am,' he broke in smoothly. 'And I found your "babbling", as you call it, quite poetic.'

Unsure whether or not he was making fun of her, she let that go, and, trying to get back to the more mundane, pursued, 'I presume from what you said just now that Slinterwood is somewhere near Mirren.'

'Slinterwood is *on* Mirren.'

'Sorry?'

He repeated, 'Slinterwood is *on* Mirren.'

Still unsure if she had heard correctly, she echoed, '*On* Mirren?'

'That's right.'

She caught her breath, bowled over by the thought of actually staying on Mirren.

For as long as she could remember, she had felt a strange affinity with the place, a secret fascination that almost amounted to an obsession.

She had thought of it as *her* island.

It drew her, called to her. Even when she and her parents had been living in Jersey, Mirren had often been in her thoughts.

Having decided to go back to Kelsay to take care of her great-grandmother, she had made up her mind to ask the old lady—who had lived within sight of the island all her life—to tell her everything she knew about it.

But on the day before Jenny's arrival another stroke had left her namesake partially paralyzed and unable to speak coherently.

Now fate seemed to be offering a chance, not only to learn something about her island, but to *live* on it for a while.

She could barely restrain her surprise and delight.

Giving her a sidelong glance, he commented, 'You look pleased.'

Steadying herself, she said, 'I am rather.'

'And surprised?'

'That too. For one thing, I thought Mirren was still privately owned.'

'It is.'

So if he rented a house there, even if it was through an agency, he probably knew the name of the family who owned it.

She waited hopefully, but, when he volunteered no more information, unwilling to appear over-curious in case it stalled the conversation she refrained from asking.

No doubt she could broach the subject again, when they had got to know each other better.

Her restraint was rewarded when he went on, 'You said, "For one thing"... So what was the other?'

'I hadn't realized there were any buildings on the island, apart from the castle.'

'Oh, yes.'

'So where is Slinterwood, exactly?'

'It stands overlooking the sea, about a mile south of the castle.'

'How strange I never saw it.'

'Not really. I'm half convinced that, like Brigadoon, it's enchanted, and only appears from time to time...'

He sounded perfectly serious. But when she glanced sideways at him she saw the corner of his long, mobile mouth twitch.

'Apart from that, until you actually reach it, it's hidden by a curving bluff and a stand of trees.'

'Is it the only house on the island?'

'No. There's a couple of farms, and about half a mile down the coast from Slinterwood there's a small hamlet that was built in the eighteen hundreds to house the estate workers.'

Seeing her puzzled frown, he went on, 'You wouldn't have

noticed it—because of the lie of the land it's only visible from the seaward side.'

'Oh… Do people still live there?'

'Yes. Though the castle itself is no longer inhabited, the estate still needs its workers, most of whom have lived on the island for generations.

'Though, of necessity, the young, unmarried ones leave to look for partners, there's something about Mirren that seems to draw them back, and keeps the cycle going.'

He relapsed into silence, leaving her to mull over what she had learnt, which was both thrilling and a little disturbing.

Thrilling because she would be living on her dream island and working for a famous author. Disturbing because—though Michael Denver had told her from the beginning that he liked to work in 'comparative isolation'—she was just starting to appreciate exactly how isolated they would be, and to wonder, with the faintest stirring of unease, if she had been wise to come.

Slinterwood, it appeared, was on the opposite side of the island to the causeway, which meant that once she was there it was a long way back.

Added to that, the causeway itself, which for part of the time would be under water, was well over a mile long and only safe to cross at low tide and in good weather conditions. So with no transport of her own, she would be a virtual prisoner.

Oh, don't be so melodramatic! she scolded herself. All it amounted to was that she and Michael Denver were bound to be thrown together a good deal in relative isolation.

But so what? A man of his standing was hardly likely to turn into a Jekyll and Hyde, or prove a threat in any way. And though the house *was* isolated, there must be a housekeeper or a manservant, someone to take care of the place and look after Michael while he was there.

But would he expect *her* to provide some companionship for the odd times he wasn't working?

It was a bit of a daunting prospect.

Though with his reputed aversion to women, he would hopefully prefer to spend his leisure time alone.

If by any chance he didn't… Well, she had taken on the job, and if providing some companionship while he was at Slinterwood proved to be a part of it she would just have to cope.

After all, she was getting very well paid. And if, at the end of a month, she wasn't happy with her duties, she could always say so and let someone else have the post.

Her thoughts busy, for the past few miles Jenny had been staring blindly into space, but now, her immediate concerns shelved, she was able to give her attention to the scenery.

They were travelling through pleasant rolling countryside where, in the shade, the grass was still stiff and white with frost, and the skeletal trees stood out black and stark against the pale blue of the sky.

Topping a rise, they ran into a small sunlit village with old mellow-stone cottages fronting a village green.

Standing opposite a duckpond, where a gaggle of white geese floated serenely, was a black and white half-timbered inn called the Grouse and Claret.

'I thought we'd stop here for lunch,' Michael said. 'If you're ready to eat, that is?'

'Quite ready. I didn't have any breakfast.'

'Why not? Pushed for time?'

She shook her head. 'To tell you the truth, I was a bit nervous.'

He found himself wondering about that rather naive statement. Had it been made for effect? To encourage him to think she was sweet and innocent?

When, his face cool and slightly aloof, he made no comment, she regretted her impulsive admission and wished she had simply said that she was hungry.

He drove through a stone archway into the cobbled yard of the inn, and, stopping by a stack of old oak beer barrels, came round to open her door.

Well, whatever faults he might prove to have, she thought as she climbed out, his manners, though quiet and unobtrusive, were flawless.

With the kind of surety that made her guess he had stopped here before, he escorted her through the oak door at the rear, and into a black-beamed bar where a log fire blazed and crackled cheerfully.

The bar, its low, latticed windows tending to keep out the sunshine, would have been gloomy if it hadn't been for the leaping flames. It was empty apart from a broad-faced, thick-necked, cheerful-looking man behind the bar, and two old cronies in the far corner who appeared to be regulars.

The landlord's hearty greeting proved Jenny's supposition to be correct.

'Nice to see you again, Mr Denver.'

'Nice to see you, Amos.'

'Me and the wife have been wondering if, the next time you came, Mrs Denver might be with you?'

Jenny saw Michael's jaw tighten, but his voice was still pleasant and level as he asked, 'And what made you wonder that?'

'Why, the newspaper stories that you and 'er were getting together again. You must have seen them.'

'I never look at the papers,' Michael told him. 'Half the stuff they print is suspect, to say the least. It pays not to believe a word.'

Amos grunted his agreement. 'We might not have done, but it sounded as though it was Mrs Denver herself who had told the reporters.'

'Well, whoever told them, there's not a word of truth in it,' Michael said shortly.

With an unexpected show of tact, Amos changed the subject to ask, 'So what's it to be? Your usual?'

At Michael's nod he enquired, 'And what about the young lady?'

'Miss Mansell is my new PA,' Michael answered the man's unspoken curiosity.

Then giving Jenny a questioning glance, he asked, 'What would you like to drink?'

As she hesitated, wondering what he would consider suitable, he suggested, 'A glass of wine? Or would you prefer a soft drink?'

Fancying neither, and having noticed a sign over the bar that announced, 'We Brew Our Own Ale', she abandoned the idea of 'suitable' and said, 'If it's all the same to you, I'd like half a pint of the home-brewed ale.'

'An excellent choice,' Amos said heartily. Then to Michael, who had managed to hide his surprise, 'No doubt you've been singing its praises.'

'I don't need to,' Michael answered gravely. 'I'm convinced that Miss Mansell can read my mind.'

'Dangerous thing, that,' the landlord remarked with a grin as he drew two half pints of ale. 'I'm only pleased my wife can't read mine. Though, mind you, she makes up for it by reading my letters and going through my pockets...

'Now then, you'll be wanting a good hot meal?'

'If that's possible?'

'It certainly is. My Sarah has her faults, but she's an excellent cook. I can recommend the rabbit casserole and the apple pie. If the young lady wants something lighter, we can always run to a salad.'

Used to Claire, who had needed to rigorously watch her diet, Michael turned to Jenny and lifted a dark, enquiring brow.

'The casserole and the pie sound great,' she said, surprising him yet again.

'Then make that two, please, Amos.'

Nodding his approval, Amos disappeared in the direction of the kitchen while, frowning a little, Jenny found herself having second thoughts.

Her new boss had obviously been a little startled by her robust choices, and she wondered if, in order to create a good impression, she should have gone for a more ladylike salad and a soft drink.

Oh, well, it was too late now to worry about it.

He carried both their glasses over to a table by the fire, and was about to settle Jenny in one of the comfortable, cushioned chairs when, seeing the firelight flicker on her face, he made to move it back. 'That might be too close for you…'

'No… No, it's fine.'

Hearing the hint of surprise in her voice, he explained, 'I suppose I got used to my ex-wife. She never liked to sit close in case the heat ruined her skin.'

When he said nothing further, deciding he was disinclined for conversation, Jenny turned her head and watched the leaping flames while she slowly sipped her drink.

Lifting his own glass to his lips, Michael found himself wondering why on earth he was talking about Claire, when for months he had done his best to avoid mentioning her name or even thinking about her.

Perhaps it was Amos's revelations that had brought his ex to the forefront of his mind.

He had little doubt that Claire's talk with the reporters had been deliberately staged. Though he was sure she no longer loved him, and probably never had, he knew that she couldn't bear to let go any man that she had once considered hers.

But she was wasting her time. He hadn't the slightest intention of taking her back. In the short time they had been married she had cuckolded him and almost succeeded in emasculating him.

Anything he had once felt for her had long since died, and when the divorce had been finalized, mingled with the pain and bitter disillusionment had been relief.

Unconsciously, he sighed, and with a determined effort he brought his mind back to the present.

His companion was sitting quietly staring into the fire. Watching the pure line of her profile, he noted that though she *appeared* to be at ease, she wasn't nearly as composed as she looked.

He was still studying her surreptitiously when their food arrived, and he suggested, 'Tuck in.'

It looked and smelled so appetizing that, in spite of her previous misgivings, when a generous plateful was put in front of her Jenny obeyed.

It was every bit as good as the landlord had boasted, the tender meat served with small, fluffy dumplings, a selection of root vegetables, and rich, tasty gravy.

Michael noted that she ate neatly and daintily, but with a healthy appetite. After getting used to seeing Claire toy with a salad and then leave half of it, he found it a pleasure to lunch with a woman who obviously enjoyed her food.

The pie that followed was just as good, with light, crisp pastry, tangy apples cooked to perfection, and lashings of thick country cream.

When Jenny had finished the last spoonful, she sat back with a satisfied, 'Mmmm…'

Watching her use the tip of a pink tongue to catch an errant speck of cream, he felt a sudden fierce kick of desire low down in his belly, and was forced to glance hastily away.

Since his divorce he hadn't so much as looked at another woman, and that sudden, unbidden reaction threw him off balance.

Seeing she was looking at him, and hoping his tension didn't show, he asked unnecessarily, 'I take it you enjoyed the meal?'

'It was absolutely delicious. I can quite see why you like to stop here—'

All at once she broke off, flustered, wondering if he'd thought her greedy.

She was trying to find some way to change what had become an uncomfortable subject when the landlord appeared to clear away the dishes and bring the coffee, sparing her the need.

'A grand meal, Amos,' Michael said heartily.

He sounded sincere, and, realizing that he too had enjoyed it, Jenny relaxed. Perhaps, because of what she saw as the newness and possible fragility of the relationship, she was simply being over-sensitive.

'I haven't tasted anything as good as that since I was here last.'

'I'll tell Sarah,' the landlord promised. 'She'll be pleased.'

For a little while they sipped their coffee without speaking, and, a quick glance at her silent companion confirming that he was once again in a brown study, she seized the opportunity to watch him.

His dark hair was thick and glossy, still trying to curl a little in spite of its short cut, and, though he lacked either charm or charisma, his face was interesting, lean and strong-boned, with a straight nose and a cleft chin.

It was the kind of face that wouldn't change or grow soft and flabby with age. At sixty or seventy he would look pretty much as he looked now.

His eyes were handsome, she conceded, long and heavy-lidded, tilted up a little at the outer edge, with thick curly lashes. His teeth too were excellent, gleaming white and healthy, while his mouth had a masculine beauty that made her feel strange inside.

Dragging her gaze away with something of an effort, she studied his ears, which were smallish and set neatly against his well-shaped head. A far cry from the large, sticky-out ears Laura had predicted.

Jenny was smiling at the remembered picture when he glanced up unexpectedly.

As he watched the hot colour rise in her cheeks, pointing to her guilt, she saw his eyes narrow.

He obviously thought she had been laughing at him, and, knowing how fragile a man's ego could be, she braced herself for an angry outburst.

But, his face showing only mild interest, he suggested blandly, 'Perhaps you'd allow me to share the joke?'

Seeing nothing else for it, she drew a deep breath and admitted, 'I was smiling at the mental picture my flatmate had painted of what you, as a successful author, ought to look like.'

'Oh? So what *should* a successful author look like?'

She repeated as near as she could remember word for word what had been said that morning.

His face straight, but his green eyes alight with amusement, he said quizzically, 'Hmm… Large, pointed, sticky-out ears… So how do I compare? Favourably, I hope?'

She smiled, and, relieved that he'd taken it so well, dared to joke. 'Not altogether. After seeing some old reruns of *Star Trek,* I've developed a passion for Mr Spock.'

Her lovely, luminous smile, the hint of mischief, beguiling and fascinating, hit him right over the heart, and for a moment that vital organ seemed to miss a beat.

Striving to hide the effect her teasing had had on him, he pulled himself together, and complained, 'Being compared to Mr Spock and found wanting could seriously damage my ego.'

'Sorry,' she said, with mock contrition. 'I wouldn't want to do that.'

'So you weren't suggesting that my ears aren't as exciting as a Vulcan's?'

'I wouldn't dare.'

'I should hope not.'

His sudden white smile took her breath away and totally

overturned her earlier assessment that he lacked either charm or charisma. Obviously he had lashings of both, hidden beneath that cool veneer.

All at once, for no reason at all, her heart lifted, and she found herself looking forward to the days and weeks ahead.

CHAPTER THREE

WATCHING her big brown eyes sparkle, Michael thought afresh how lovely she was.

He had been in Jenny's company now for several hours, and ought to be getting used to her beauty, almost taking it for granted.

But he wasn't.

In fact, just the opposite.

The fascination the first sight of her had aroused was still there, and growing stronger.

Which was bad news.

The last thing he wanted or needed was to be attracted to his new PA. That would be the ultimate irony, as Paul would be quick to point out.

That morning, when Paul had phoned to find out the result of the interview and Michael had admitted that Jennifer Mansell was on a month's trial, Paul had been quietly jubilant.

'I'm sure that in spite of all your doubts she'll prove to be just what you need.'

'We'll see,' Michael said cautiously. 'It depends on what kind of woman she turns out to be, and how I get on working with someone else.'

Paul grunted. 'Well, of course I can't answer for the latter, but, so far as Miss Mansell's concerned, I've heard nothing but good about her.

'Though I'll keep my ear to the ground, just in case, and if I *do* hear anything further I'll let you know. In the meantime stop being such a misogynist and give the poor girl a chance.

'She's known to be good at her job, and, as I said before, I don't think she's the kind to throw herself at you. If by any chance she does, for heaven's sake take her to bed. It might be just what you need to turn you back into a human being.'

'Thanks for the advice,' Michael said dryly, 'but I've had my fill of women.'

Now he found himself wondering how he would react if Jenny Mansell *did* throw herself at him.

So far she'd given not the slightest sign of wanting to do any such thing. Rather, she had trodden warily, as though negotiating a minefield, looking anything but comfortable whenever the conversation showed signs of straying into the more personal...

Becoming aware that time was passing, he swallowed the remains of his coffee and remarked, 'If you're ready, we really ought to be on our way.'

Jenny, who had been sitting quietly watching his face, wondering what he was thinking, said, 'Yes, I'm quite ready.'

'There would be no hurry if we didn't need to be over the causeway before the tide turns.'

His words reminded her of her earlier doubts about the advisability of being so isolated, and perhaps some of that uncertainty showed on her face because, frowning, he queried, 'Is there something wrong?'

She hesitated. If she did still have doubts, common sense told her she should voice them now, before it was too late...

He was watching her face, concerned that for some reason she was going to back out at the last minute, and his voice was tense as he demanded, 'Well, is there?'

She lifted her chin, and, knowing that she was going anyway, regardless of doubts, answered, 'No, there's nothing wrong.'

'Then perhaps you'd like to freshen up while I pay the bill? I'll see you back at the car.'

As Jenny washed her hands and tucked a stray hair or two into the silky coil she rationalized her decision by telling herself that, having come this far, had she confessed to doubts he would have had every right to be angry.

She had a feeling that, in spite of his offer of a month's trial period, he hadn't been particularly keen to engage her in the first place, so he might have been glad of the opportunity to send her packing back to London.

Then not only would she have missed her chance to stay on Mirren, but it would have meant losing a job she'd really wanted without even starting it, and never seeing Michael Denver again.

The latter shouldn't really matter.

But somehow it did.

Though she was too aware of him to be altogether at ease in his company, she wanted the chance to get to know him better, to find out for herself just what kind of man he was, what made him tick.

When she made her way outside, he was waiting to settle her into the passenger seat.

The sun, though low in the sky, was still shining, but already the air seemed chillier, less clear, promising the onset of an early dusk.

'How long before we get to Mirren?' she asked as they left the Grouse and Claret behind them and headed for the coast.

'Half an hour or so.'

Unwilling to ask direct questions, she suggested innocently, 'Perhaps you could tell me something about the island?'

'What do you know already?'

'Apart from what I saw on that one short visit, and what

you've already told me, nothing, really. I only know that it's always fascinated me.'

'Well, it's roughly nine miles long by three wide. The higher ground is interspersed with pasture land, and, apart from some stands of pines, the only trees are the ones around Slinterwood.

'Because the island has fresh water springs, it's been inhabited for centuries, and for most of that time it's been home to a rare breed of sheep similar to merinos, prized the world over for their fine, soft wool.

'These days a lot of the farmland has been turned into market gardens, which produce organic fruit and vegetables for the top London hotels.'

With a slight grin, he went on, 'At the risk of sounding like a guidebook, I'll just add that on the seaward side there are some pleasant sandy coves, ideal for summer picnics and swimming.'

'It sounds lovely.'

'It's certainly picturesque.'

She waited, hoping he'd tell her more about his connection with the island, and about the family who owned it.

But he changed the subject by remarking, 'One good thing about travelling at this time of the year is that there's not too much traffic.'

There proved to be less as they approached their destination. Even in high summer this part of the coast was relatively quiet, and now the coastal road was deserted in both directions as they joined the rough track that led down to the causeway.

Glancing at the water, Michael remarked, 'The tide must have turned some time ago.'

'How can you tell?' she asked.

'At low tide there are sand flats on either side of the causeway. Now they're almost covered, which means we're only just in time to get across.'

She felt another little shiver of pure pleasure at the thought of staying on the island she had always considered to be a special, enchanted place.

In the meantime, the here and now was magical. The early evening air was quite still, the water flat calm, the raised causeway, a shining ribbon edged by black and white marker poles, curled into the distance, where Mirren seemed to float, serene and enchanted, on a sea of beaten silver.

Dusk was already creeping in, veiling a sky of icy pearl with delicate wisps of grey and pink and the palest of greens.

Jenny found herself holding her breath as they started across the causeway, almost expecting the island to retreat before them like some mirage.

They were nearly halfway across when a slight change in the lie of the land brought into view the twelfth-century castle. Its towers and battlements silhouetted against the sky, it seemed to be part of the craggy outcrop of rock on which it stood.

As it had on her first visit, the sight brought a strange surge of emotion, and, feeling as if her heart were being squeezed by a giant fist, she sighed. It must have been wonderful to have lived there.

As though reading her thoughts, Michael remarked, 'It seems a shame that the castle is no longer inhabited.'

'Perhaps it's unsafe?' she hazarded.

He shook his head. 'Though the stone is crumbling a little in parts, it's still structurally sound.'

So *why* wasn't it still lived in? she wondered.

The question trembling on her lips, she glanced at him, but something about his hard, clear-cut profile, the set of his jaw, convinced her that she had asked enough questions for one day, and, biting it back, she returned her attention to the view.

Leaving the causeway, where the impatient tide was already lapping at the marker poles, Michael took the road that she had driven up all those years ago.

Having reached the castle and passed the spot where she

had parked previously, they carried on up the winding road, skirting a high bank on the right.

Growing on the rocky bank amongst the dried bracken were a straggle of gorse bushes, some of which were in full bloom.

As they drove up the hill, in the nearside mirror Jenny caught a glimpse of Mirren Castle from a new and intriguing angle, and asked impulsively, 'Would you mind very much if we stopped for a moment? I'd like to take a closer look at the castle.'

'Of course not.' He brought the car to a halt and climbed out to open her door. Then together they walked back a few yards to a natural vantage point.

The air was bitingly cold, and even in so short a time the sky was starting to lose its colour and get hazy, while a bank of cloud had appeared on the horizon behind the castle.

'It looks so different from here,' she exclaimed, after she'd studied it for a moment or two. 'I hadn't appreciated that the rear walls were built on a cliff that drops straight into the sea. It must have made it much easier to defend.'

'It was a virtually impregnable fortress in its day. The enemy got through its outer defences only once and that was due to an act of betrayal…'

Eager to hear more, she turned to look at him, her face expectant.

'One of the defenders, who had been bribed by the besieging army, crept down at night and raised the portcullis. But he didn't live to benefit from his treachery. It seems he was one of the first to be killed before the enemy were driven out.'

Seeing her shiver in the thin air, he broke off and said briskly, 'You're cold. We'd better get moving.'

As they walked back to the car, noticing the yellow gorse flowers glowing eerily now in the gathering dusk, she remarked wonderingly, 'Isn't it amazing how anything can bloom in such bitter weather?'

Reaching to open the car door, he said, 'Luckily, gorse blooms all the year round.'

She glanced up at him. 'Luckily?'

'Surely you've heard the old saying, "When gorse is in bloom, kissing's in season"?'

She smiled, and, glancing up to make some light remark, saw the sudden lick of flame in his eyes and read his intention.

But trapped between the car door and his tall, broad-shouldered frame all she could do was stand gazing up at him, her big brown eyes wide, her lips slightly parted, her wits totally scattered.

As he bent his dark head and kissed her mouth her eyes closed helplessly, shutting out the world and leaving only sensation.

Just at first his lips felt cold, then the coldness turned to heat as his mouth moved lightly against hers, making every nerve-ending in her body sing into life and sending her head spinning.

Though Jenny had been kissed many times, and though most of those kisses had been long and ardent, somehow they had failed to move her, leaving her feeling untouched, aloof, uninvolved.

Andy's kisses had been pleasurably different and exciting, yet even they had left some small part of her vaguely dissatisfied.

But while Michael's thistledown kiss couldn't have lasted more than a few seconds, by the time he lifted his head her legs would no longer hold her and her very soul seemed to have lost its way.

Opening dazed eyes, she became aware that he was half supporting her, and made an effort to find her feet and stand unaided.

Though he too had been knocked sideways, partly by her response, and partly by a torrent of feeling that had almost swept him away, his recovery was light years ahead of hers.

Cursing himself for a fool, he stepped back.

He hadn't meant it to happen. Kissing her had been a sudden impulse that he knew he ought to regret.

But somehow he couldn't.

Though if her office reputation was anything to go by, she should be angry at the liberty he'd taken, more than ready to slap him down.

But a quick glance at her face showed that she looked neither. She still appeared dazed, as if that kiss had shaken her as much as it had shaken him.

Seeing that she was starting to shiver, he opened the car door and, a hand beneath her elbow, helped her in.

Without a word, she sat down and fumbled for her seat belt. She still hadn't fastened it by the time he slid behind the wheel, and he leaned over to fasten it for her.

As his muscular thigh accidentally pressed against hers, though she said nothing, he felt her instinctive withdrawal.

While he started the car and put it into gear, Jenny made an effort to pull herself together and make sense of her feelings.

After all, what had happened really? Just a light, casual kiss to illustrate an old saying. A kiss that had clearly held no importance for him.

Yet remembering that little lick of flame in his green eyes before he had kissed her, she wondered if it *had* been quite that casual. Or had it been a preliminary? A chance to test the water, so to speak?

Though from what she'd heard, she had formed the distinct impression that after his disastrous marriage Michael Denver was reluctant to have anything to do with the female sex. And the vibes she had picked up during the interview had gone to support that.

Recalling how his jaw had tightened as though he was in pain when the landlord of the inn had mentioned his ex-wife and the likelihood of a reconciliation, she wondered if perhaps he still loved her.

From all accounts *she* had been the one to stray, and perhaps, when it was too late, she had found herself regretting that lapse.

After all, she had opposed the divorce. And she must believe he still loved her, or she wouldn't have talked to the press about the possibility of them getting back together.

True, he had denied it, but maybe it was only his hurt pride and anger that had so far prevented him from taking her back? Or maybe he was simply teaching her a lesson?

If he was, *while* he was, he might need a woman in his bed. Sex without strings or commitments, simply to assuage a natural appetite?

But in these days of sexual freedom and equality, many women felt the same.

And why not?

Except that personally she couldn't embrace that way of thinking. So if Michael Denver *was* hoping for someone to keep his bed warm while he was away from London—and that could account for the very generous salary—she might have a problem.

It was a far from reassuring thought, and she began to wish that she hadn't accepted his offer.

'Another minute or so and you'll be able to see Slinterwood Bay.' His quiet remark broke into her uneasy thoughts.

His tone was so down-to-earth, so mundane, that all at once her vision of having to fight him off dissolved into the absurd.

Talk about letting her imagination run away with her! It was just as well he didn't know what she'd been thinking, otherwise he would be wondering what kind of madwoman he had hired as his PA.

Still berating herself, she turned her attention to the scenery once more.

They had breasted the rise and were following the coast road that curled round behind the bluff. On their left the dimpled sea was spread like a sheet of pewter in the silver-grey dusk, the tide creeping up the smooth expanse of sand and eddying between low outcrops of rock in the small bay.

The sky was still clear enough to catch a glimpse of a thin

silver crescent of moon, while far out to sea a bank of purple cloud formed a mountain range on the horizon.

'And there's Slinterwood itself.'

In a sheltered hollow at the foot of the hills, a stand of mixed trees, some deciduous, some coniferous, curved a protective arm around a long, low, creeper-clad house.

Wisps of pale smoke were curling lazily from two of its barley-sugar chimneys and hanging in the still air like twin genies.

Surrounded by a low-walled terrace, the house was built of stone, with crooked gables, overhanging eaves, and dormer windows. It looked as if it had stood in that spot since time immemorial.

On the seaward side, stone steps ran down to the beach where, well above the high-water mark, a small blue and white rowboat had been turned upside down.

They took the track through the trees that led to the front terrace, and came to a halt by an old oak door with a lighted lantern above it.

Jenny smiled. With an arched top, black iron studs and hinges, and wood bleached to a pale, silvery grey, it was the kind of enchanted door that was familiar from childhood fairy tales.

Either side of the door were long windows made of small, square panes of glass, the edges encroached on by trails of ivy.

When she had gathered up her coat and bag, Michael helped her out, before retrieving her case.

He appeared to have no luggage of his own, but of course, as he came here regularly, it would be like a second home.

Lifting his head, he asked, 'Can you feel how still it is?'

And it was. Nothing moved in the blue-grey dusk. Not a single twig stirred, not an ivy-leaf quivered. Everything was so calm and motionless it was as if the very air held its breath in anticipation of the coming night.

'Winter evenings on Mirren often bring this kind of still-ness,' he added as they made their way over to the door.

Jenny had half expected the housekeeper to be waiting, but when no one materialized, apparently unsurprised, Michael produced an ornate key and turned it in the huge iron lock.

Then, swinging open the heavy door, he switched on the lights and ushered her into a panelled hall that ran the entire width of the house.

There were doors to the right and left, and at the opposite end—like a mirror image of the landward side—were a matching door and windows that looked towards the dusky sea.

The wide floorboards were of polished oak, and on the right a dark oak staircase climbed up to the second floor.

Since drawing up outside, and seeing that fairy-tale door, Jenny had felt as if she knew the place. Now, as she stepped over the threshold, she had the strangest feeling that she had been here before. That the old house had been waiting for her return, and welcomed her back.

Catching sight of her expressive face, Michael asked, 'What is it?'

'Nothing…' Seeing he wasn't convinced, she admitted, 'I just had the strangest feeling that I know the house. That it's familiar…'

He set her case down, and without believing it for an instant suggested, 'Perhaps you've been to Slinterwood before?'

'No, I'm sure I haven't. It must be déjà vu.'

Yet though she was quite certain she had never been here before, the feeling of warmth, of being made welcome, of coming home, persisted.

Michael, who had always believed that houses had their own aesthetic or emotional effect or appeal, an atmosphere that anyone sensitive could pick up as vibes, asked carefully, 'This feeling… Is it an unpleasant one?'

'No… No, anything but.'

'But quite strong?'

'Yes. Very.'

'When you say you feel you know the house, can you visualize the layout of the rooms?'

'No… I don't think so…'

Something impelled him to say, 'Try.'

Standing quite still, she closed her eyes. 'The doors on the same side of the hall as the stairs lead to a big living-kitchen and… I suppose you'd call it a morning room.

'Next to the kitchen there's a walk-in larder that has a green marble cold-slab, and a deep porcelain sink with an old-fashioned water pump over it.'

'Go on,' he ordered tersely.

With no idea where she was getting such clear mental pictures, she obeyed. 'Across the hall, there's a long living-room on the seaward side, and behind that a library-cum-study and a dining-room.'

'What about upstairs?'

Opening her eyes, she said, 'I'm not sure… I think there's a master bedroom above the living-room, and several smaller bedrooms with fireplaces, sloping ceilings, and polished floorboards.

'At the end of a corridor, there are two steps down to a big, old-fashioned bathroom, with a claw-footed bathtub…'

A curious note in his voice, he said, 'And you think that's an accurate description of the rooms?'

She shook her head with a self-deprecating smile. 'I'd be very surprised if it were.'

'Why?'

'Well, either it's complete guesswork, or it's something I've dreamt at one time or another.'

Though she tried to keep it light, the clearness and certainty of those mental pictures had shaken her somewhat.

With no further comment, he picked up her case and turned

to lead the way up the stairs and along a corridor with polished oak floorboards.

'I understand from Mrs Blair that she's put you in the lilac room.'

He slanted her a quick glance, as if he expected some comment, but all she could think of to say was, 'That sounds lovely.'

It was a pleasant room on the seaward side of the house, with light, modern furniture, pale lilac walls, white paintwork and, rather to her surprise, an en-suite bathroom.

Except for the sloping ceiling, the polished oak floorboards and scattered rugs, it wasn't at all what she had visualized.

Knowing he was watching her face and aware of the relief she couldn't altogether hide, she observed, 'There's no fireplace.'

His voice level, he told her, 'At one time there were fireplaces in all the rooms. But apart from the one in the main bedroom, they were taken out some three or four years ago when oil-fired central heating and en-suite bathrooms were put in.'

'Oh,' she said, a shade hollowly.

Putting her case on an oak blanket chest, he offered, 'Before you make yourself at home, I'll show you the rest of the upstairs.'

Opening doors and switching on lights as they went, he told her, 'Next door is my room…'

The main bedroom was a large, attractive room with a black-beamed ceiling, polished period furniture, and a stone fireplace, in which a log fire had been laid ready.

'And across the landing,' he went on, 'there are three smaller bedrooms, pretty much the same as yours, and a bathroom.'

The bathroom, which was at the end of a short corridor and down two steps, had a claw-footed bathtub, just as she had described.

Seeing he was waiting for her to say something, she offered as carelessly as possible, 'A lucky guess.'

Though he frowned a little, he made no comment.

As they went back across the landing he suggested, 'When you've had time to freshen up, come down and we'll have a cup of tea before I show you round the rest of the house.'

Nodding her thanks, she returned to her room, where she gnawed her lip thoughtfully.

Common sense told her that it was silly to find herself still wondering if she'd been here before, when she knew quite well she hadn't.

So where had those vivid mental pictures come from?

Having seen the outside of the house—with its steep gables and plethora of chimney pots—the fireplaces and sloping ceilings were a logical deduction. While the position of the bathroom, and the steps leading down to it, *must* have been just a lucky guess.

But although she did her utmost to explain away what had happened, the feeling of *knowing* the house still persisted.

Oh, well, she thought, it was a warm, friendly feeling, so she wouldn't worry about it.

When she had washed her hands and tidied her hair she descended the stairs and crossed the hall, still with that feeling of being at home, and opened the living-room door.

It was a long spacious room with pale walls and a beamed ceiling, comfortably furnished and homely, as she had known it would be. It was lit by a couple of standard lamps and the glow of a log fire.

Pulled up to the hearth were two soft leather armchairs, and on a low table between them was a tray of tea and a plate of what appeared to be home-made scones, with small dishes of jam and cream.

Glancing up from the chair he was occupying, Michael invited, 'Come and join me.'

Once again rocked by the impact the sight of him always had on her, she obeyed, and, taking a seat opposite, remarked, 'Though the whole house is anything but cold, this is really cosy.'

'So long as the electric pump's working, the central heating keeps the place at a comfortable temperature,' he agreed.

'Strictly speaking,' he went on, 'the fires are only necessary when the electricity supply fails. But I love an open fire, especially in the winter.'

'So do I,' she agreed wholeheartedly.

'Why?'

'Why?' she echoed uncertainly.

'Yes, why?'

'Well, I—I find a fire is visually pleasing. It brings a room to life…'

'Go on.'

Somewhat fazed by his persistence, she attempted to put her feelings into words. 'As far as I'm concerned, a fire meets some primitive need that's made up of more than just the requirement for warmth.'

It was so close to his own feelings—feelings that Claire had neither understood nor shared—that he was taken aback, But all he could find to say was, 'Very nicely put.'

Unsure whether or not he was mocking her, and deciding to change the subject, she asked, 'Would you like me to pour the tea?'

'If you wouldn't mind,' he agreed smoothly.

Outwardly serene, she assembled fine china cups patterned with a ring of tiny flowers, and reached for the matching teapot. 'How do you like your tea?'

'A little milk, no sugar.'

Watching her calm face and graceful movements, he frowned a little. She both puzzled and intrigued him. The fact that she knew the house had taken him by surprise, and he wanted to see into her mind, to know how she had managed to come by such detailed knowledge and information.

There had to be some explanation, and sooner or later he would find it, he promised himself as, with a word of thanks, he accepted the cup and saucer she passed him.

Taking a sip, he added, 'It's nice to be waited on occasionally.'

Deciding to play the gracious hostess, if that was what he wanted, she offered him a plate and a scone.

His face straight but his eyes amused, as if he knew exactly what she was thinking, he accepted the plate and took a scone.

Watching her replace the rest, he queried, 'Won't you join me?'

As she started to shake her head he added persuasively, 'Mrs Blair is proud of her scones, and quite rightly.'

'They look very tempting,' Jenny admitted. 'But I don't think so.'

'Why not?' Recalling Claire's horrified expression when he'd suggested that she try one, he added, 'You're not worried about a few extra calories, are you? You're plenty slim enough.'

'No... Luckily I have the right kind of metabolism, so I don't need to worry about putting on weight. It's just that I had such a big lunch.'

'So did I. But we can't hurt Mrs Blair's feelings.'

He smiled at her, a white, slightly crooked smile that put fascinating creases beside his mouth, lit up his face, and warmed his green eyes. 'Tell you what, shall we share one?'

Beguiled by his smile and that teasing glance, and wondering how she could ever have thought him unattractive, she found herself agreeing. 'Why not?'

He split the light, floury scone in two and spread both halves with jam and a generous amount of cream, before cutting each piece into four quarters.

Then on an impulse, he picked up one of the pieces and reached across to offer it.

Without conscious volition she opened her mouth, and he fed it to her.

Thrown by the gesture, she sat like someone in a dream and watched him eat his own piece.

The little ritual was repeated until the scone was all gone.

Though she had told herself it was nothing, and tried to appear calm and unmoved, something about the unexpected intimacy had made her feel hollow inside, and her hand was shaking slightly when she lifted her cup to her lips.

CHAPTER FOUR

WATCHING Jenny, and seeing the slight flush on her cheeks, Michael wondered what on earth had impelled him to act in that way.

But whatever it had been her reaction had proved surprising. Any other newly hired PA would have either backed off or made a big deal of it.

She had done neither.

Though clearly taken by surprise, she had met the informality with a kind of sweet, slightly shy acceptance that he had found oddly moving.

Now she was avoiding his eyes, looking anywhere but at him, and he noticed that the hand holding her teacup wasn't quite steady.

He was wondering how best to restore the status quo when the lights flickered and seemed momentarily in danger of going out.

'It looks as though the generator is on the blink again,' he remarked, 'which can be a nuisance when I'm working.'

'It must be,' she agreed in a heartfelt voice.

'If the story's flowing,' he went on, 'I hate to be held up. That's one of the reasons I decided I needed a PA who can take shorthand.'

'Does it go on the blink often?'

'From time to time it gets temperamental and leaves us in the dark.'

Which no doubt accounted for the oil lamps she had noticed scattered around. 'And you've only that to rely on?'

''Fraid so. At the moment there's no national-grid electricity on the island. Nor are there any phone lines. Plans are under way to have both by next year, but at the moment a mobile is essential.'

'Oh, dear!' she exclaimed. In the excitement and the rush to get ready, she had left hers on charge.

'You have a problem?'

'It's only that I've just realized I've forgotten to bring mine.'

'Is there anyone you need to get in touch with?'

She half shook her head. 'Not at the moment. I left a note for my flatmate… It's just that I feel lost without my mobile.'

'Well, if the need arises, you can always borrow mine. More tea?'

'No, thanks. What about you?'

He shook his head, and, keen to see her reaction to the rest of the house, suggested, 'Shall we continue the tour?'

She rose and accompanied him to a door at the far end of the room that led through to a red-carpeted library-cum-study.

It was a large, handsome room with book-lined walls and a wide stone fireplace, in which a fire had been laid ready.

The fireplace itself was ornate, the stone surround decorated with mythical birds and beasts. In the centre of the mantel was a symbol she knew well, a phoenix rising from the ashes.

Perhaps that in itself wasn't remarkable.

What *was* remarkable was that she had *known* it was there even before she'd looked.

A little shiver ran down her spine.

But she was making too much of it, she told herself sturdily. That kind of ornamentation was no doubt quite common. She could almost have expected it.

Realizing that Michael was waiting for her, she pulled herself together and prepared to move on.

He opened a communicating door, and ushered her through. 'At one time this was the dining-room, but it was so little used that I decided to make it into an office.'

It was clear that she had been mistaken in presuming he just rented the house. To be able to make that kind of major alteration, he must surely own it.

The office was sparsely furnished and businesslike, its windows fitted with slatted blinds. There was a smoke-grey carpet, a large desk on which sat a computer and a printer, a black leather swivel chair, a bookcase full of what appeared to be reference books, and a filing cabinet.

With no ornaments or pictures, it was clearly intended as a place to work without any distractions.

Leaving by a door on the far side, they crossed the hall and went through into a large living-kitchen, with comfortable-looking rustic furniture and a big, wood-burning range.

'As you can see, it's been brought up to date fairly recently,' Michael remarked.

Looking at all the mod cons, which included a microwave and a dishwasher, Jenny asked, 'And there's no problem with the power?'

'So long as everything isn't switched on at the same time, the generator, which is housed through here—' he let her peep into what had once been a stable block and was now garages '—manages to cope.

'Next door to the kitchen is the cold larder, which has been left more or less as it was…'

If the kitchen hadn't disturbed her serenity, the larder did. There were the shelves and cupboards, the green marble slab at the far end, and the deep porcelain sink with its old-fashioned water pump, just as she had visualized it.

'And it fits your description perfectly,' he went on softly, 'even to the pump.' Then, like a cobra striking, 'Do you think it works?'

'Oh, yes,' she said with certainty.

'You're quite right. But how did you know?'

Thrown, she stammered, 'Well, I—I didn't really.'

But when he'd asked the question, she had pictured clear water gushing from the spout when the handle was pumped up and down.

Until then she had been trying to treat the whole thing lightly, as though it was some game. Now the *strangeness* of it threw her, making her feel nervous, unsure, as though she were stranded on thin ice that might give way at any moment and plunge her into dark and unknown depths.

His eyes on her face, he queried, 'And you're *sure* you've never been here before?'

'Positive.'

She looked and sounded genuinely shaken, and for a moment he was almost tempted to believe her. But only for a moment, then common sense returned, making him wonder what kind of game she was playing.

After his divorce, some women had gone to great and diverse lengths to capture his interest, but none as intriguing or as well planned as this.

But how *could* she have planned it?

To have come up with such an accurate description of the house, she must have been here before, seen photographs of the place, or been told all about it. And she hadn't known where he was taking her until the very last minute.

Perhaps Paul had mentioned that he did his writing at Slinterwood, and given her detailed information about the place?

Knowing Paul, that didn't seem very likely, but it was the only logical explanation he could come up with. Unless she was clairvoyant.

'Perhaps you have second sight?' he suggested, half in earnest.

A little flustered by the concept, she assured him, 'No, not that I know of. But if I believed in reincarnation, I might think I'd lived here in some previous life.'

'And do you? Believe in reincarnation, I mean?'

'No.'

'So how do you account for it?'

She couldn't.

But still she tried. 'When I've had the chance I've always enjoyed visiting National Trust properties and stately homes... All I can think is, I must have seen, and half remembered, another house enough like Slinterwood to superimpose the two.'

It sounded weak even in her own ears, and a little defensively she said, 'I'm afraid it's the only explanation I can come up with.'

'There *could* be another one,' he mentioned, his voice even.

When she looked at him uncomprehendingly, he went on, 'Paul knows Slinterwood quite well—perhaps he told you all about it?'

She shook her head. 'No.'

Then, catching the fleeting expression of doubt that crossed his face, she added sturdily, 'You can ask him if you don't believe me. I'd never even *heard* of Slinterwood until you mentioned it earlier today.'

There was an unmistakable ring of truth in the words that brought him up short, and he found himself saying quietly, 'I do believe you.'

She relaxed a little as they moved on and came to a halt outside the final door.

'What you thought might be a morning room is actually the housekeeper's room. Or should I say it used to be, when there was a housekeeper.'

'But I thought... You mentioned a Mrs Blair. Isn't *she* the housekeeper?'

'Mrs Blair is the wife of one of the estate workers, and lives in the hamlet just down the coast. She cleans and airs the place when I'm in London and gets everything ready for when I'm coming down, while her son does the heavy work and takes care of the generator.

'But once I'm here I prefer to look after myself without interruptions, so she doesn't come in unless I ask her to.'

'Oh… Oh, I see…' Jenny said, all her previous doubts about the wisdom of being isolated here with him—especially now she'd discovered they were quite alone—flooding back.

He smiled a little, as if reading her thoughts, and assured her, 'Don't worry, even if we are here all by ourselves I'm not going to turn into an axe murderer or a dangerous psychopath.'

She flushed. 'I didn't think you were.'

And it was true. After her reaction to that earlier kiss, and the shared intimacy by the fire, her worries were of a different nature.

Once again reading her mind with deadly accuracy, he queried, 'But you do have other concerns?'

'Other concerns?' she echoed. Then hastily, 'No! No, certainly not.'

'Well, in that case,' he said blandly, 'I'll leave you to unpack and settle in while I make a phone call or two.'

Jenny climbed the stairs, her thoughts chaotic. Had she been wise to say she had no other concerns? After all, it could be interpreted in two ways.

Normally both her brain and her tongue were well coordinated and under control, but Michael Denver had the disturbing ability to scatter her wits and turn her into a gibbering idiot.

Thinking back to the original interview, she had foolishly stated, 'A good PA should do whatever it takes to keep her boss happy.'

Suppose he'd taken that to mean she was willing to share

his bed? If he had, and he turned up the heat, where would that leave her?

Here. Quite alone with him. And vulnerable.

It wasn't that she was afraid he might overstep the mark. What shook her was the sudden realization that he might not need to, that it wasn't so much *him* she wasn't sure she could trust as *herself.*

But surely she would only have to remind herself of the past, of her humiliating failure at relationships, to enable her to keep the barriers firmly in place?

While she had waited for the right man to appear, she had been more than able to keep other males at bay with a cool reserve that had effectively frozen them off.

Then Andy had come along.

He had seemed to be the one, and, their wedding only a few weeks away, she had given in to his pleas to sleep with him.

Until the flat they were planning to rent became vacant, Andy had been sharing a flat with a man named Simon. A small flat with paper-thin walls and very little privacy.

Knowing that Simon might walk in at any moment had put Jenny on edge, and, despite Andy's assurance that his flatmate 'wouldn't give a toss', she had been unable to relax.

Though she had tried very hard to please him, to be everything he had wanted her to be, the experience had left her feeling bitterly disappointed and woefully inadequate.

She had hoped that Andy would understand and be patient. But, showing a less than pleasant side of his nature, a side she had never seen before, he had accused her of not caring enough, of lacking warmth and passion and being next door to frigid.

That night, back in her own bed, she had cried herself to sleep.

The following morning, rallying a little, she had tried to tell herself that things would improve once they were in their own flat and married.

But her confidence, both in herself and in Andy's professed love for her, had been badly shaken.

Then, not long afterwards, and quite by chance, she had discovered that he was two-timing her.

Their flat had finally been vacated, and she had been taking some things round when she had discovered him in what would have been their bed, with another woman, and the bottom had dropped out of her world.

She had thrown his ring at him, and, feeling used and betrayed, hurt and humiliated and bitterly angry, vowed never to trust another man.

Laura, ever practical, had said, 'You should thank your lucky stars that you found out what the swine was really like before you married him.'

While recognizing the sense of that, it had still taken her months to get over the hurt, to claw back some of her pride and self-respect, and bury her feelings of inadequacy.

So how could she think of herself as *vulnerable* when it came to a man like Michael Denver? A man who, apart from one brief kiss, had really shown no interest in her as anything other than his hired PA.

Yet somehow she did.

It made no sense, but that one light kiss had moved her in a way that no other man's kisses had.

Though that didn't mean she had to act like a complete numbskull, she scolded herself. She'd always been very successful at masking her feelings, a trait that had helped her enormously when it came to dealing with difficulties in either her personal or professional life, and that was what she would do with Michael, at least until she got her newly awakened libido under control!

Having succeeded in convincing herself that she'd been fretting over nothing, she pushed any remaining worries to the back of her mind, and, closing the heavy curtains to shut out the darkness pressing against the panes, set about unpacking.

Putting her nightdress and dressing gown on the end of the bed, she stowed the rest of her things neatly away in the wardrobe and the chest of drawers, while she debated changing out of the suit she was wearing.

A lingering caution suggested she should stick with the businesslike image. But while she could see the sense of that, she felt the need to change into something easier, slightly less formal.

Having decided, she stripped off the suit and hung it in the wardrobe before freshening up in the pretty lilac and white bathroom.

Then, making a positive statement, she chose a simple olive-green dress that Laura had disgustedly described as 'matronly', and slipped it on.

Somehow she had to get through their first evening alone together with the guidelines firmly in place and her composure intact.

Hopefully he would want to begin work as soon as dinner was over—she grasped at the prospect like a lifeline—and once their attention was fixed firmly on his next book it should make things a lot easier.

When she descended the stairs and made her way to the living-room, she found it was empty. Which might possibly mean he was already in his office working.

But that too was empty, as was the library.

She finally ran him to earth in the kitchen where, his sleeves rolled up and a tea towel draped around his lean hips, he was using two wooden spoons to toss a green salad.

The oak table was already set with a fish platter, a bowl of what looked like home-made dressing, and a basket of crispy rolls. A bottle of white wine waited in a cooler.

Glancing up from his task, he said, 'Two things. I hope you like fish?'

'Yes, I do.'

'And I hope you don't mind eating in the kitchen?'

'No, not at all.' Glancing at the glowing range, which had been set in an inglenook fireplace, she observed, 'It's nice and homely.'

'I decided to keep the old range to sit in front of, and cook on if the generator fails.'

Her hair, he noted, was still in the businesslike coil and her dress, with its long sleeves, calf-length skirt and demure neckline, clearly wasn't intended to be provocative.

It didn't look as if she had any plans to vamp him, he thought with wry humour.

But though the dress was conservative, it was far from dull. The silky material clung lovingly to the curve of her bust and waist, and swirled becomingly around her slender legs when she moved.

Aware of his scrutiny, she asked quickly, 'Is there anything I can do to help?'

According to Claire, most women disliked having to get their own drinks, and, deciding to put her to the test, he suggested, 'Perhaps you wouldn't mind getting us both a drink?'

A loaded drinks trolley was standing to one side, and while she surveyed the various bottles he watched her.

When her inspection was over, appearing completely unfazed, she queried, 'What would you like?'

'A dry Martini with ice and lemon, please.'

'Shaken not stirred, presumably?'

He grinned. 'What else?'

Spooning crushed ice into a silver cocktail shaker, she teased, 'Your middle name doesn't happen to be James, by any chance?'

His face straight, so that she didn't know whether or not to believe him, he told her, 'As a matter of fact it does.'

With a composure that suggested she knew exactly what she was doing, she added measures of vodka and French vermouth to the ice and shook it thoroughly, before pouring the mixture into two Martini glasses and adding a twist of lemon to each.

Handing him one, she suggested, 'Try this and see if it's to your taste.'

'Thanks.'

As he accepted the glass their fingers brushed and a kind of electric shock tingled up her arm.

She had read about that effect in romantic novels, but had never believed it could happen in real life. Now, as she found it could, her composure abruptly deserted her.

He made no comment, but the gleam in his eye told her he knew.

When he'd taken a sip of the cocktail, he said, 'Spot on.' Then, with a lopsided grin, 'You may have just added bartender to the other things I expect my PA to do.'

She couldn't help wondering exactly what he meant by 'other things', but was too chicken to ask.

There was a pair of rocking chairs in front of the range with a low table between them, and, trembling inside, her legs none too steady, she took her own glass and went to sit by the fire.

When the salad was mixed to his satisfaction, he discarded the tea towel and joined her by the fire.

Glass in hand, he leaned back comfortably, his legs crossed neatly at the ankles. 'The meal's ready, but if you're in no hurry...?'

'Well, no, I'm not... But I—'

'Then I suggest we relax for a while and get to know one another.'

Judging by the expression on her face, Michael thought, she didn't welcome his suggestion.

That impression was amply confirmed when she hurried on, 'I thought you might want to eat straight away so you could work later?'

'No. I wasn't thinking of doing any work tonight.'

'Oh…' she said, her lifeline gone and her heart sinking. Then rallying, 'So what time will you want to start in the morning?'

He shook his head. 'I won't. After the pressures of London life, I usually take a day or two to relax and unwind while I mull over my next plot.'

'Oh,' she said hollowly.

If only he *would* get down to writing in earnest, she thought in helpless frustration. As soon as he had made a start and his book was absorbing all his attention, she would feel a great deal happier.

'And one of the best ways to do that, I find, is to go walking.'

Well, at least he'd be out.

'Do you like walking?'

Ambushed by the question, she answered truthfully, 'Yes.' Adding, 'Before I went to live in London I used to walk for miles along the beach—' Suddenly realizing where her answer might be leading, she broke off abruptly.

But her anxiety was put at rest when he merely said, 'Of course, at this time of the year it depends to a great extent on the weather. Rain's forecast, so if it happens to be heavy it might be expedient to find some other form of relaxation.'

The prospect of him ending up housebound because of the weather wasn't one that pleased her.

His face straight but a hint of amusement in his voice, he observed, 'You seem positively disappointed at the thought of not starting work straight away.'

She blurted out the first thing that came into her head. 'I— I've never worked for a writer before and I can't wait to see how a book comes to life, and to know I'm playing some small part in its creation.'

Then grasping at what, hopefully, would be a safe topic, she asked, 'Do you begin by plotting out the various chapters?'

Normally he never discussed his writing with anyone, but

as they were going to be working together he decided to go along with it.

'No. I usually start with just a bare idea of the storyline. Then I concentrate on the characters, and their relationship to one other.

'Once I have those things clear in my mind, I start to make preliminary notes.

'If it begins to gel, I'm under way. If it doesn't, I start all over again…'

She soon found herself fascinated by what had begun as a mere expedient, and listened eagerly.

Although the conversation wasn't going along the lines he had planned, responding to what he recognized as a genuine and intelligent interest, Michael answered her questions freely.

Though she hadn't stated as much, from the questions she asked it soon became clear that she had read his books.

More than read them—*knew* them.

By the time he paused to suggest that it might be time to eat, Jenny had forgotten both her motive for starting the conversation and her earlier agitation.

When she was seated, he helped her to a selection of seafood and some of the crisp salad before pouring wine for them both.

While they ate a leisurely meal he kept the conversation light and impersonal, and she relaxed even more.

By the time they returned to sit in front of the stove with their coffee, she realized that their first evening alone together was almost over.

Though she was too conscious of him to be totally comfortable, she had not only survived the day, but in some respects thoroughly enjoyed it.

Their cups were empty, and she was about to mention that she would like an early night when, out of the blue, he remarked, 'I find it almost impossible to believe that a beautiful woman like you has no man in her life.'

When, flustered, she said nothing, he fished, 'But possibly you haven't met the right one yet?'

Uneasy about the direction the conversation was taking, but feeling the need to say something, she admitted, 'I was once engaged to be married.'

'Oh, when was that?'

'It ended six months ago.'

'May I ask what happened?'

Endeavouring to hide the feelings that, in spite of all her efforts, were still somewhat painful, she said flatly, 'I gave him back his ring when, a few weeks before we were due to be married, I found him in bed with another woman.'

'So presumably you don't believe in…shall we say…open-ended relationships?'

'I have some friends who do, but that kind of relationship isn't for me.'

'Even if you really loved the man?'

'*Especially* if I loved him.'

'And you haven't met anyone you could fall in love with since your engagement broke up?'

'No,' she answered.

Then before Michael could delve any further, she put her cup on the low table and rose to her feet. 'Now if you'll excuse me, it's been a long day, and last night I didn't sleep very well…'

It was the truth. Anxious about the forthcoming interview, she had been unable to settle, and had tossed and turned for a long time before finally falling into an uneasy doze.

'So I'm really tired,' she added.

He was about to try and persuade her to stay when, seeing her stifle a yawn and noticing that there were faint blue shadows beneath her eyes, he uncoiled his long length and agreed, 'Then bed it is.'

This wasn't at all what she had planned, and, disconcerted, she blurted, 'Oh, please… Don't let me disturb you.'

'You're not. I was rather looking forward to a reasonably early night, myself.'

The ground cut neatly from beneath her feet, she had no choice but to let him escort her upstairs, switching out lights as they went.

At her bedroom door he paused, and, blocking her way, stood looking down at her.

Taking a deep, unsteady breath, she stammered, 'Well, g-goodnight.'

Putting a single finger against her cheek, he said, 'Goodnight. Sleep well.'

As, his light touch rooting her to the spot, she gazed up at him like a mesmerized rabbit, he bent towards her.

The conviction that he was about to kiss her again galvanized her into action, and, flinching away, she brushed past him and fled into her room, followed by the sound of his soft laughter.

Once inside, her heart racing, her breath coming fast, she leaned weakly against the door panels. A moment later she heard his light footsteps move away, and then the door of his room close.

Angry with herself, and even angrier with him when she recalled that mocking laughter, she wished fervently that, rather than panicking and running away, she had kept her head.

She should have stood her ground and made it plain that she had simply come here to do a job and wasn't in the market for a bit of light dalliance. Instead she had acted like a silly, immature schoolgirl.

But then that was the effect Michael Denver had had on her from the start.

She groaned inwardly. However was she going to face him in the morning?

But even as she quailed at the prospect, she realized that something about the little scene that had just taken place didn't quite add up.

Michael was a skilful, sophisticated man, not an inexperienced youth liable to dither, and there had been ample opportunity, not only for him to kiss her, but to start a big seduction scene if he'd really wanted to.

So why, instead of just getting on with it, had he telegraphed his intention?

Had he wanted to see her reaction?

Or had the whole thing been just a charade, a deliberate attempt to fluster her?

Oh, come on! Common sense stuck in its oar. Why should he *want* to fluster her?

Wasn't she, once again, letting her imagination run away with her? Wasn't it much more likely that she had been totally mistaken? That he hadn't intended to kiss her at all?

If she *had* misinterpreted what had been just an innocent movement on his part, and bolted, no wonder he had laughed.

She groaned again. It was a toss up which of the scenarios was worst, she thought as she picked up her nightie before heading for the bathroom to clean her teeth and prepare for bed.

Perhaps, in the morning, after making such a fool of herself, it might be better to tell him that she had had second thoughts and wanted to leave?

But did she really want to leave Slinterwood?

The answer had to be no.

Though the strange rapport she felt with the house made her extremely reluctant to leave it, she was forced to admit that the overriding reason for wanting to stay was Michael Denver himself.

Being in his company wasn't altogether comfortable, but it gave her a buzz, sharpened her perceptions, and made all her senses diamond-bright.

Love was supposed to have the same effect, she mused as she stepped out of the shower and began to dry herself. But though she had thought herself in love with Andy, he had never made her feel so aware, so *alive*.

Perhaps she had been turned on by the thought of working for a writer of Michael's calibre?

She had certainly *wanted* the job, but what she hadn't bargained for was her unprecedented reaction to the man himself.

Though surely she could keep that under control? she thought as she pulled on her nightdress.

Admittedly she had made a poor job of it so far, but the first day was over, and from now on things should get easier. All she needed to do was keep cool and not let him fluster her.

CHAPTER FIVE

JENNY awoke next morning to find it was almost nine o'clock. After lying awake for several hours the previous night unable to stop thinking about what a fool she'd made of herself, she had overslept.

It was just as well Michael didn't want to start work immediately.

Jumping out of bed, she drew aside the curtains and looked out of the window at the lovely, peaceful scene spread before her.

The sea resembled a slightly wrinkled sheet of silver paper with a lacy edging of filigree where the waves washed gently up the pale sand.

For as far as she could see in either direction the beach was deserted, the only sign of life a grey cormorant standing on one of the rocky outcrops, spreading out its wings to dry.

Despite the fact that rain had been forecast, the sun was shining and the sky was a clear baby-blue.

With a bit of luck, she thought, Michael Denver might take himself off for a long walk.

But even if he did, she would have to face him first, and, remembering his mocking laughter, she found it was a daunting prospect.

What was she to say to him? How could she excuse her stupid behaviour?

The answer was, she couldn't.

However, knowing it was no use putting off the evil moment, she went purposefully into the bathroom to clean her teeth and shower.

Having dressed for the day in tailored fawn trousers, a donkey-brown blouse and flat-heeled pumps, she coiled her hair, applied a little make-up and sallied downstairs before her courage failed her.

She found him in the kitchen breaking eggs into a pan. An appetizing smell of coffee and grilling bacon filled the air.

'Good morning.' His tone was measured, his manner practical, down-to-earth. There was no sign of the mockery or derision she had half expected.

Even so, she was unable to meet his eyes as she responded with a polite, 'Good morning.'

Noting that evasion, and guessing the cause, he smiled inwardly.

Last night, at her bedroom door, he had been very tempted to kiss her again, but then, reminding himself of all the problems such a move could cause, he had drawn back.

That hesitation had given her the chance to step in and show her true colours, but instead of reacting seductively her response had been to bolt like a startled rabbit.

Which could mean one of two things. Either she was as innocent and naive as she appeared, or she was playing some deep game.

Abandoning the puzzle for the time being, he asked, 'Sleep well?'

She picked up the slightest hint of amusement in the question—as if he already knew the answer—but, choosing to ignore it, she lied, 'Yes, very well, thank you.'

'If you'd like to sit down and pour the coffee, breakfast is almost ready.'

As she obeyed he queried, 'How do you like your eggs? Sunny side up? Or asleep?'

'Asleep, please.'

'Same here.' Expertly flicking fat over the yokes, he added, 'But then I was already sure that our two hearts beat as one.'

Her hand shook a little and some of the coffee she was pouring spilt into the saucer.

'Damn,' she muttered.

Hiding a smile, he turned away to dish up the crispy bacon and perfectly cooked eggs.

They ate without speaking, and only when Michael removed their empty plates to stack in the dishwasher did she find her voice and say, 'Thank you. That was very nice.'

'Toast and marmalade?' he offered.

'No, thanks, I've had quite enough.'

Resuming his seat, he refilled their coffee cups and observed, 'The rain seems to be holding off, so I think a good long walk is indicated.'

Unsure whether or not he was including her, and reluctant to say anything in case he hadn't been and she put the idea into his head, she made no comment.

A moment later he settled the matter by saying, 'It might be a good idea to bring your notebook and pencil just in case I need any notes taking.'

Then, catching sight of the expression on her face, 'You *did* say you liked walking?'

'Yes.'

'So you have no objection to accompanying me?'

Unable to think of a convincing reason to back out, after a moment or two she answered, 'No.'

If he noticed her brief hesitation, he gave no sign. 'Then I'll pack a spot of lunch while you get your outdoor things. It's much colder than it looks, so wrap up well.'

Up in her room, she pulled on a pair of sturdy shoes, found

a sweater to wear beneath her coat, and a woolly hat to pull down over her ears. She did enjoy walking, and at least being out in the open air and on the move would be preferable to staying cooped up indoors with him. And it would give her a chance to see something of her island.

When she descended the stairs she found he was waiting in the hall, also dressed for walking, and with a rucksack on his back.

Running an eye over her sensible shoes and clothing, he nodded, before asking, 'Any preference as to which direction?'

She shook her head. 'No, I'll leave it to you.'

'You mentioned that when you lived at Kelsay you used to enjoy walking along the beach...'

Surprised that he'd remembered, she said, 'Yes.'

'Then I suggest we follow the coastal path down as far as Gull Point, before striking inland and taking a shorter route back.'

'That sounds fine,' she agreed.

Grinning, he said a shade sardonically, 'Heaven be praised, an amenable woman!'

'Quite a lot of us are.'

'Not in my experience.'

'Then you've obviously been associating with the wrong kind of women.'

The teasing retort was out before she could prevent it, and, wondering what on earth had made her blurt out something that sounded so rude and insensitive, she bent her head and waited for the storm that was bound to come.

But all he said was, 'You may well be right.'

In spite of feeling she had got off to a bad start, Jenny found the walk both pleasant and invigorating. The heavens were cloudless, the scenery picturesque, and the salty tang of the sea air a long-missed and well-remembered pleasure.

Breathing in the cold air was like drinking sparkling champagne, and the light had that clear, diamond-edged sharpness that only winter days brought.

For the first hour or so they walked in silence, keeping up an easy pace that covered the miles seemingly without effort.

During that time, Michael had been trying to think up some interesting characters to people the plot that had begun to unfold in his mind. But more often than not his attention, rather than focusing on his book, had wandered to the woman by his side.

Though Jenny appeared to be quiet and reserved, she was far from dull, and she certainly didn't lack spirit. Yet when, after that first impulsive kiss, he had expected some display of coldness or anger, she had appeared dazed, quiescent.

Which failed to add up.

As did her pre-knowledge of Slinterwood.

Though even if they *were* both imponderables at the moment, there were bound to be answers…

But there he was, doing it again!

For the umpteenth time, he lassoed his straying thoughts, and, annoyed by his inability to concentrate, told himself irritably that he should never have engaged a PA. Particularly a female one, and, more especially, a female who intrigued and distracted him.

Unconsciously taking out his displeasure on her, he quickened his pace.

After half a mile or so, it became plain that she was having a struggle to keep up with him, but not a single word of complaint passed her lips.

Feeling like a heel, he slowed down and suggested, 'Shall we have ten minutes' rest and a cup of coffee?'

Sounding a little breathless, she said, 'A cup of coffee would be lovely.'

He led the way to a nearby outcrop of flattish rock, and, taking a Thermos from the rucksack, filled two cups and handed her one.

As they drank she asked, 'Any idea about the storyline yet?'

'The beginning of one,' he admitted grudgingly.

'What about the characters?'

He shook his head, his dissatisfaction with himself plain. 'I was wondering…'

Though he asked, 'What were you wondering?' his tone didn't sound as if he would welcome suggestions.

Though she doubted the wisdom of going on, having stuck her neck out, she felt she had no choice. Taking a deep breath, she asked, 'Have you ever considered carrying any of your previous characters over to another book?'

His attention caught, he queried, 'If by any chance I did, which of the characters would you advocate?'

Her face eager, she said, 'Two that I found particularly fascinating were Finn and Dodie…'

She had named two minor characters from his third novel, *Rubicon,* the fate of whom, to suit the plot, had been left deliberately vague and inconclusive. Characters he had often thought he could have done a great deal more with.

'I've always wondered what happened to them after they left Orlando.'

The fact that she had spoken about them as if they were real people set off fireworks in his mind and sent his thoughts racing.

Watching his face grow aloof and distant, and only too aware of the lengthening silence, she lost countenance and said, 'I—I'm sorry. Please forgive me. I should have kept my suggestions to myself.'

'Far from it!' he exclaimed jubilantly, and, removing the empty cup from her nerveless fingers, set it down, and, taking her face between his palms, kissed her full on the lips. 'You've given me just the idea I needed.'

When he released her, flushed and breathless, she stammered, 'Oh… W-well, I only hope it works.'

'It'll work,' he told her with certainty.

Shaken by that kiss, but warmed by the thought that she'd been able to help in some small way, she watched him pack away the cups and the flask.

Shrugging the rucksack into place, he said, 'I suggest we have lunch at Gull Point, but first, as a reward, I'll take you to a secret cave with an answering echo.'

That day set the pattern for the days that followed. A stationary high pressure system kept the weather fine and dry, and while the book began to take shape they walked the length and breadth of the island.

Though Jenny ventured no further suggestions, rather to Michael's surprise he found himself talking to her about the emerging plot, finding it an advantage to have an intelligent listener to bounce his ideas off.

The days spent walking in the open air working up an appetite were followed by good and substantial evening meals.

Michael had been in touch with Mrs Blair, and while they were out that good lady made a daily visit to tidy up, lay the fires, and replenish the fridge.

Each evening, after their return, they would sit down to a pre-dinner drink and decide on a menu. At Jenny's suggestion, they now took it in turns to make dinner, and he was pleased to find that she was an excellent and inventive cook.

Dinner over, they spent their evenings by the fire, sometimes talking, sometimes reading, sometimes in what passed as a companionable silence.

On the surface everything appeared to be calm and contented, but beneath the surface there were still disturbing eddies and undercurrents.

Though Jenny *appeared* to be as ideal as Paul had suggested, along with his unanswered questions and reoccurring doubts Michael was struggling against a growing physical attraction that he was finding hard to control.

He tried to tell himself that it was nothing serious, simply a normal male's sexual response to a beautiful, desirable female, and that any other woman might have caused the same response.

But remembering the many attractive women who had vied for his attention after his divorce—all of whom had left him cold—somehow he didn't believe it.

Since that last, impulsive kiss, well aware that it would be playing with fire, he had been careful not to touch her, not even to let their fingers accidentally brush when he handed her a drink.

For her part, still plagued by that disturbing sexual awareness, and knowing how vulnerable she was, Jenny was grateful for his restraint.

Then the weather changed abruptly. Storm clouds rolled in over the sea, and that day, having walked the more hilly centre of the island, they were forced to battle their way back through heavy rain and a raging wind.

That evening it should have been Jenny's turn to cook, but seeing how tired she was after changing into dry clothes Michael had sent her to sit in front of the range while he made a seafood risotto.

Her hair was still damp, and she had left it loose around her shoulders. It made her look about sixteen, he thought, and even more appealing.

After the meal they sat by the fire, sipping coffee and talking desultorily while they listened to the rain beating against the windows and the soughing of the wind in the chimney.

To all intents and purposes it was a quiet, contented, domestic scene.

A few weeks ago that thought would have made him laugh cynically. But now, to his surprise, rather than hating to have someone else here he was starting to look forward to the quiet evenings spent in Jenny's company.

He watched her face in the flickering firelight. Her eyes were half closed, and between softly parted lips he caught the gleam of pearly teeth.

His pulse rate quickening, he was forced to look away while he searched for some safe topic of conversation that would steer him well away from temptation.

By nine-thirty, noticing that she was having to stifle her yawns, he suggested that they both needed an early night.

She rose at once, and, having escorted her upstairs, Michael said an abrupt, 'Goodnight,' and disappeared into his own room before he gave way to the urge to kiss her.

Wondering at that sudden curtness, she went through to the bathroom to clean her teeth and shower.

Over the past week, though still plagued by that unbidden attraction and unable to totally relax, she had found the time spent in Michael's company both exciting and rewarding.

Though things had got off to a rocky start, she was beginning to feel that she had made the right decision after all, and to hope that by the time the month's trial period ended he might feel the same.

If he didn't, she knew she would be desolate.

She derived an immense amount of pleasure and satisfaction from the fact that he discussed his book with her and, from time to time, not only asked her opinion but appeared to listen to it.

Added to that she loved the island and the house, and knew that she would be happy to stay here in this lovely place for as long as he wanted her to.

Though they had covered a lot of ground there was still a great deal more to see, including a closer look at the castle, and she hoped that the storm would blow itself out before he began to work on his book in earnest, and they were tied to the house…

Her thoughts still busy, she had just returned to the bedroom when, without warning, the lights went out, plunging her into total darkness.

She had got used to the city, where there was always some degree of illumination, and the sudden complete absence of light came as a shock.

Taking a deep breath, she stood and waited for her eyes to adjust to the dark.

They didn't, and she soon realized that they weren't going to. The blackness was total. It wrapped her up and pressed against her suffocatingly, making her blind and helpless.

As though the absence of sight sharpened her other senses, she became aware of sounds that previously had stayed in the background—waves surging up the beach and crashing onto the rocks, wind buffeting the house, and rain lashing against the windows.

Enjoyable sounds, had she been tucked up cosily in bed. Not quite so enjoyable when she was standing in utter darkness, unsure of which way to move.

It had been a long and strenuous day, and, feeling bone-weary, she thought longingly of getting into bed and going to sleep, so that the absence of light wouldn't matter.

She made an effort to visualize the room before moving carefully towards where she thought the bed ought to be.

Only it wasn't.

There seemed to be a great deal more floor space than she remembered.

Altering direction, she tried again.

After another couple of fruitless attempts, totally disorientated, she admitted that she hadn't the faintest idea where the bed was.

If she could find a wall and follow it round... One hand held out in front of her, she began to move forward cautiously.

She had gone only a few steps when she stumbled into something she identified as the dressing-table stool, and knocked it over with a clatter.

As she fumbled to set it upright there was a light tap and

the door opened. 'Having problems?' Michael's voice queried out of the darkness.

Her heart leapt in her chest, and even in her own ears her voice sounded husky and breathless as she answered, 'I was trying to find the bed, but I got disorientated and knocked over the dressing-table stool.'

'I know exactly where the dressing-table is,' he said reassuringly, 'so stay where you are, and I'll come and get you.'

Apart from the faint brush of his bare feet on the boards, he moved silently, and a few seconds later she jumped as an unseen hand took hers.

He must have eyes like a cat, she thought as he began to lead her unerringly through the blackness.

Wits scattered by his touch and his nearness, it took her a little while to realize that they had left her room and were heading down the corridor.

At the same instant that realization dawned she saw the half-open door of the next room illuminated by a reddish-gold glow.

'Why are you taking me to your room?' she demanded, hanging back.

'It seems the most sensible place for you to wait while I have a look at the generator,' he told her in a no-nonsense voice. 'Your room will soon start to get seriously cold, and there's a fire in mine.'

He gave the hand he was holding a little tug.

Unwilling to seem foolish by arguing, she bit her lip and followed him into the cosy bedroom, where an oil lamp glowed and a cheerful log fire blazed in the wide grate.

He led her to an armchair in front of the fire and pressed her into its cushioned comfort, before releasing her hand.

Feeling curiously shaky, her own hand still tingling from the contact, she looked up at him.

He was wearing a short navy dressing gown belted around his lean waist, and that seemed to be all. Through the gaping lapels she caught a glimpse of a smooth, olive-skinned chest and the strong column of his throat.

She felt a sudden, devastating urge to put her lips to the hollow at the base, and, feeling her colour rise, she hastily lowered her eyes.

His bare legs and feet, she noticed, were strong and well proportioned, and if feet could be said to be nice his were, with straight toes and neatly trimmed nails.

Noting her gaze, he remarked lazily, 'Fascinating things, feet, don't you think?'

Blushing harder than ever, she looked away, staring with some desperation into the flames.

Taking pity on her, he stopped his teasing, and asked, 'Would you like a nightcap of some kind while you wait?'

'No, thank you.' She was well aware that she'd sounded prim.

'Well, in case a story's flowing and I can't sleep, or I wake up and want to work during the night, I've had a coffee-maker installed…'

Of course. She remembered seeing it when he'd first shown her his room.

'So when I get back, if I've managed to fix the generator, we can have a hot drink.'

Bearing in mind that this was his bedroom, it sounded too intimate for comfort, and she told him quickly, 'All I really want is to get into my bed.'

Accepting her decision with good grace, he said, 'Well, if you're okay where you are for the time being, I'll pull on some clothes and get to work.'

While she sat and listened to his quiet movements and the rustle of clothing, she stared resolutely into the fire.

A minute or so later, fully dressed and wearing a thick Aran sweater, he picked up the oil lamp and headed out, closing the door quietly behind him.

Beginning to relax, she leaned back in the chair and watched pictures in the flames while she listened to the storm.

It was warm and comfortable, and in spite of her lingering agitation the flickering firelight had a soporific effect, and after a short time her heavy eyelids began to droop.

When Michael returned, Jenny was sitting bathed in a red-gold glow, fast asleep.

Though the neckline of her ivory satin nightie was modest by modern-day standards, it allowed an enticing glimpse of the upper curve of her breasts and the start of the shadowy cleft between them.

She looked like every man's dream, lovely enough to tempt even a saint, and he felt his heart start to beat faster.

He put down the lamp, tossed aside his sweater, and, irresistibly drawn, moved closer and stood gazing down at her.

Her head was tilted a little to one side, and beneath silky brows her long black lashes lay like fans against her high cheekbones. Even in sleep the pure line of her jaw and the curve of her chin showed character and determination, but her beautiful mouth looked soft and vulnerable.

He wanted to stoop and crush it beneath his own, to take her in his arms, to carry her off to bed and make love to her. But he knew instinctively that if he did, it wouldn't be just a one-night stand.

Even though he still had to solve the puzzle of what kind of woman she was, he was beginning to feel that she was destined to play some special kind of role in his life.

Perhaps Paul had already sensed that. Paul who had sounded a little anxious when, a few minutes before the lights went out, he had phoned to say, 'I'm sorry to call so late. But I wondered how you were getting on with Jenny Mansell.'

'No real problems so far,' Michael answered cautiously. 'What makes you ask?'

'Earlier tonight I went out for drink with Peter, one of the personnel bods from Global, and heard something a bit disturbing.'

'Go on,' Michael said evenly.

'Well, as it happens, Peter's sister, Lisa, is in the same department that Jenny used to work in. Apparently, soon after she'd left, Lisa overheard one of the men telling another that Jennifer Mansell's coolness was all put on, that once she was away from the office, she was "hot stuff".

'He boasted that on quite a number of occasions she'd taken him back to her place and acted "like some sex-starved nymphomaniac".

'When Lisa, who had apparently liked Jenny, asked him why he hadn't said anything sooner, he protested that it was hardly the done thing to talk about a woman while she was still there.

'Lisa pointed out that it was hardly the done thing to talk about a woman behind her back. That shut him up temporarily. But only temporarily. Now rumours about Jennifer Mansell being predatory are rife.'

'Tell me something, do *you* believe the rumours?'

'I'm more inclined to believe that they're simply malicious, and spring from the fact that he'd made a pass at her in front of the entire office and been turned down flat. But I thought, having got you involved with the lady in question, I'd better let you know.'

'Well, thanks for the warning.'

'Sorry and all that. If there's anything I can do…?'

'As a matter of fact there is. Jenny once mentioned that she had a flatmate. Flatmates tend to know one another well, so if you could have a discreet word with her or him…?'

'Will do.'

'Oh, by the way,' Michael seized the opportunity to ask, 'when you first told her about this job, did you mention Slinterwood at all?'

'Slinterwood?' Paul sounded a bit blank. 'No, should I have done? Was there a problem?'

'No, no problem. I just wondered.'

'She didn't dig her heels in about going?'

'No, not at all. Look, I'll tell you all about it one of these days.'

'Right. I'll let you know what, if anything, the flatmate has to say.'

Frowning, Michael ended the call, his thoughts in turmoil. He didn't *want* to believe that there was any truth in the rumours. But though, up to press, she had shown not the slightest sign of coming on to him, in fact just the opposite, his brush with predatory women had made him wary.

However, sooner or later he'd find out the truth, but now he should wake her, and let her get to bed.

Thinking of Sleeping Beauty, he stooped and touched his mouth to hers.

Though her eyes remained closed, she gave a little sigh, her lips parted beneath that lightest of pressures, and her warm arms slid round his neck.

Without conscious volition, he lifted her to her feet while he deepened the kiss, and, like dropping a lighted match into a pool of petrol, passion exploded between them.

Fully awake now, and with no thought of past or future, of rights or wrongs or consequences, Jenny kissed him back, melting against him.

She was warm and fragrant in his arms, and while he kissed her his hands traced her slender curves, lingering over the enticing swell of her hips and buttocks, before following her ribcage upwards to the soft but firm curves of her breasts.

The touch of his hands made Jenny's pulse race madly and brought every nerve-ending in her body into singing life.

Through the thin satin of her nightdress his fingers found and teased the nipples, feeling them grow firm beneath his touch.

Transported by the exquisite, needle-sharp sensations he

was arousing, she began to make little mewing sounds deep in her throat.

Those sounds inflaming him even further, he slipped the satin straps from her shoulders and bent his dark head to take first one, and then the other, of the pink velvety nipples into his mouth.

As he suckled sweetly she gasped and shuddered, the acute pleasure he was giving her almost more than she could bear.

When her nipples felt seductively ripe and swollen on his tongue, he slid the nightie down over her hips and let it pool around her bare feet.

Then, her arms still around his neck, he drew back a little and looked down at her. Her cheeks were flushed and her lips gently swollen.

His eyes dropped, and in the golden glow from the dying fire he saw her naked body for the first time.

She was graceful and perfectly proportioned, with a smooth, flawless skin. Her breasts were beautifully shaped, her waist slender above nicely rounded hips, her legs long and slim as a ballerina's.

Drawing her close again, he kissed her while he stroked his hand down her flat belly to the nest of black silky curls between her thighs.

She shuddered repeatedly as his long fingers found their goal and started to explore, luring all sensation downwards.

Normally his foreplay was both skilful and leisurely, a game he enjoyed and excelled at, a game he could play until he'd driven his partner almost wild with pleasure.

But no woman had ever affected him as Jenny did, and for the first time since he was a teenager he found it almost impossible to hold back, to keep his self-control.

When the little inarticulate murmurs she'd been making changed to pleas, shaken by the depth of his longing, he lifted her in his arms and carried her over to the bed.

Pulling aside the covers, he laid her down, and, with hands

that weren't quite steady, stripped off his clothes before joining her.

She received him back silently, willingly, her arms going round his neck once more while she gladly welcomed his weight.

It was like making love to an eager flame, but after their first skyrocket trip to the stars he contrived to take it slower, delaying the climax, drawing out and intensifying the pleasure until it spilt over into ecstasy.

Temporarily spent and sated, his breath coming quickly, his heart still racing, the blood still pounding in his ears, he lay quietly.

Blissfully happy, and loving the feel of his dark head pillowed on her breast, Jenny lifted a hand and stroked his hair tenderly.

Strangely content, he lay for a while before lifting himself away. Then, turning onto his back, he gathered her close and settled her dark head at the comfortable juncture between chest and shoulder.

Nestled against him, the steady beat of his heart beneath her cheek, she was fast asleep within seconds.

He could hear her light breathing, her breath occasionally fluttering in her throat as if she was still in the grip of some powerful emotion.

Having had his fill of women, he hadn't meant to get involved, and he should be regretting what had happened, what complications might ensue.

If it hadn't been for Paul's phone call, and the doubts it had raised, he would have sworn she was inexperienced.

But whatever the truth of the matter, what they had just shared had been shared on equal terms.

Jenny hadn't sought to make the running, nor had she merely surrendered, rather she had returned passion for passion in what had seemed to be an innocent, untutored way that had shaken him to the core.

Had she been an obviously worldly woman, and anyone

other than his own PA, it would have been a sexual encounter he would never have forgotten.

As it was, with everything else that was involved in the equation, his feelings were in chaos, his well-ordered life turned upside down.

CHAPTER SIX

JENNY surfaced slowly, reluctantly, unwilling to break the spell of the previous night. Still half asleep and basking in the golden glow of the most wonderful experience of her life, she lay with her eyes closed, savouring the glory of it.

For perhaps the first time, she felt truly like a woman—contented, fulfilled, blissfully happy, as though she had finally found her heart's desire.

But as she became fully awake the reality of making love with Michael was dawning on her.

As she was shocked into complete wakefulness all the pleasure drained away, and she lay quite still, her body frozen, her mind jarred.

It was a few seconds before her brain accepted the fact that she was lying in Michael's arms, in Michael's bed.

Following her less than happy relationship with Andy, hurt, disillusioned, and bitterly humiliated, she had sworn never to get involved with another man.

Now, after months of keeping any would-be suitors at bay, she had gone to bed with her boss. A man she scarcely knew.

What on earth had made her do it? she wondered in growing horror.

Perhaps, because he had come to her and kissed her so

gently, so sweetly, her defences had been down, and before she had even started to appreciate the danger it had been too late.

Passion had flared between them, the kind of passion she had never felt before, the kind of passion that swept away any doubts or fears.

She had rejoiced in the certainty that here was the man she had been waiting for, that the two of them were meant to be lovers, meant to be together always.

But in the cold light of day she realized that that had been just a fantasy, an illusion.

In reality, passion—she shied away from the word lust— was all it had been.

In the past, when other girls had gone to bed with men they scarcely knew, she hadn't judged them, but she *had* wondered at the wisdom of their actions.

Now, without intending to, she had joined their ranks, and with a vengeance.

The whole episode had been a terrible mistake, something she could only regret.

Except that she *couldn't* regret it. It had been the most wonderful and earth-shattering experience, and she would never be the same again.

The memory of last night would stay with her for the rest of her life, even though Michael didn't care a jot for her, and had just wanted to use her.

But even as the charge went through her mind, she knew it was false. Though he couldn't possibly feel anything for her but lust, he had been tender and caring, *careful* of her…

In contrast to Jenny's slow awakening, Michael's brain was instantly alert, and even before he opened his eyes every minute of the preceding night was crystal-clear in his mind.

He hadn't meant it to happen, but he couldn't regret that it had.

Though by nature a caring, passionate man, in the past he

had found love-making satisfying and pleasurable rather than earth-shaking.

With Jenny it had been an entirely new experience. She had burnt in his arms like an eager flame, arousing a storm of feeling that had rocked him to the core.

She was like no other woman he had ever met. From the moment he'd set eyes on her she had been special, his awareness of her so intense that at times he had felt almost befuddled.

And now he had once made love to her, he knew that he wanted her, craved for her and all she could give him, as an addict craved a drug.

Though she was lying quite still, he knew that she was awake, and he wondered what she was thinking, what the previous night had meant to her.

But of course that would depend entirely on what kind of woman she really was, what she wanted from him, and how she viewed their new relationship.

Did she still want him as much as he wanted her?

He felt instinctively that she did.

But there was one way to find out.

Jenny caught her breath as the arm that was lying over her tightened, and a warm hand closed lightly around her breast and began to stroke and tease the nipple into life.

She wanted to ask him to stop, to tell him that though she'd been foolish enough to let last night happen, it didn't mean that she was prepared to go on with it. But her heart was in her mouth and the words wouldn't come.

He raised himself up on one elbow, and his lips brushed her shoulder before travelling up the side of her neck.

As she shivered in response he turned her onto her back and smiled down at her.

In the morning light that filtered through the closed curtains, she could see the creases either side of his mouth, the gleam of his white teeth, and the intriguing cleft in his chin.

He appeared fresh and vital, in spite of the dark stubble that adorned his jaw.

'You look beautiful,' he told her softly, 'all warm and seductive, just slightly tousled, and still flushed with sleep.'

He bent and touched his lips to hers.

His breath was fresh and clean, and though she longed to kiss him back she didn't want to be just his plaything, someone who filled a need while he was away from London.

Summoning all her will power, hoping to freeze him off, she kept her mouth firmly closed.

When he gave a slight sigh and lifted his head, she thought she'd succeeded.

But wanting, *needing,* to make her his again, to make her come to life and respond as completely and passionately as she had done the previous night, he returned to lay siege.

For a while his mouth played with hers, stroking, sucking, nibbling, bestowing little plucking kisses that coaxed and titillated and demanded a response.

A response she tried hard to withhold, and couldn't.

When her lips finally parted helplessly beneath his, he gave a little murmur of satisfaction and deepened the kiss, making her forget everything but the here and now, the delight and excitement his mouth was engendering.

Then his hands began to caress her, and in no time at all she was lost, mindless, any urge to resist swamped by the passion he was so easily arousing.

Using first his fingers, and then his mouth—the slight rasp of his stubble against her soft skin adding extra stimulation—he teased her nipples into life and found erogenous zones she hadn't even been aware of, before his hand slid down to the warmth of her inner thighs to bestow fresh delight.

The earlier urgency gone, he took his time about pleasuring her, finding his own pleasure in her little gasps and moans, and the knowledge that her body was so responsive to his touch.

Time and time again she thought herself sated, but each time he skilfully rekindled her desire, until finally he moved over her and joined her on that roller-coaster ride to the stars.

When she awoke for the second time she was alone in his bed. A fire was blazing in the grate, and above the sound of the wind and rain beating against the windowpanes she could hear the shower running and a faint, but tuneful whistling.

Her thoughts chaotic, she struggled to find some kind of mental stability and not condemn herself too much for what had just happened.

When she failed miserably on both counts, she bowed to the inevitable and admitted that she had made a complete hash of things.

Instead of freezing him off, she had kissed him back and triggered off a further bout of love-making that had shattered her good resolutions.

Though in the past she had never had to question her self-control, when it came to Michael she had thought of herself as vulnerable.

And rightly so.

He affected her like no other man she had ever met, and had he felt anything for her beyond lust she would have stayed for as long as he wanted her.

But he didn't.

Which made the situation impossible.

The only thing she could do was to leave.

Closing her mind to the fierce stab of pain that decision brought, she did her utmost to concentrate on practicalities.

He hadn't been planning to start work today, so she would ask him to take her over to the mainland, where she could get some transport back to London.

Then the following morning she could call at her nearest employment agency and start looking for another position.

As if nothing had happened.

Whereas *everything* had happened, and she would never be quite the same again.

When, on her return home, she told Laura her flatmate would be both surprised and shocked.

Shocked, not for any moral reasons, but simply because she had known Jenny for long enough to be certain it wasn't in her nature to go to bed with a man she hardly knew, and her boss into the bargain.

Many a time, since her engagement had ended, Laura had urged her to loosen up, to find another boyfriend and have some fun.

'All this holding back gets you nowhere,' she said flatly. 'In fact that's probably what drove Andy to cheat on you in the end.'

Then quickly, 'Sorry, I shouldn't have said that.'

'Why not?' Jenny asked a shade bitterly. 'I've no doubt you're quite right.'

'Then why don't you let your hair down next time you meet a man you like? Live a little while you're still young?'

But with her own firmly entrenched standards of morality, Jenny found herself unable to follow that advice.

Laura's comment was, 'I can't say I expected you to. I only hope Mr Right comes along before you get too old and withered to make the most of it.'

However, nothing had been said about the possibility that Mr Right, when he *did* come along, might not fit into the role…

Becoming belatedly aware that the shower had stopped, and Michael might be back at any moment, Jenny slipped out of bed and, seizing her nightdress, which had been draped over a chair, was hurrying to the door when his voice stopped her in her tracks.

'Don't go…'

Clutching the nightie to her, she spun round to find he was

standing there naked, his hair still damp, his jaw smoothly shaven, a towel draped around his neck.

Broad-shouldered and slim-waisted, lean-hipped and muscular, his belly flat, his legs long and straight, his smooth olive skin gleaming with health, he was so superbly *male* that she could hardly breathe.

'Brunch is all ready,' he went on, 'and I thought we might have it here by the fire…'

In the circumstances, eating together in his bedroom hardly seemed a sensible option, but her tongue refused to work.

Grinning at the expression on her face, he offered, 'If it seriously bothers you, I could put on some clothes first.'

When she continued to stand there struck dumb and unable to take her eyes off him, he went on, 'On the other hand, if you keep looking at me as though I'm Suleiman the Magnificent we could end up back in bed.' A gleam in his eye, he queried, 'Which option do you prefer?'

Blushing rosily, and hastily averting her gaze, she said, 'Brunch. With both of us dressed.'

She had meant to state it firmly, but it came out more like a plea.

He sighed. 'Well, in that case I expect the pancakes will wait ten minutes.' Then teasingly, 'But I'm getting hungry, so any longer and I might have to come and fetch you.'

Without further ado, still clutching her nightie, she turned and fled.

Her feelings all over the emotional map, she showered, cleaned her teeth, and brushed and coiled her hair.

Then, unconsciously hurrying, she found fresh undies, off-white slimline trousers, a fine wool shirt-blouse in olive-green, and a pair of low-heeled court shoes.

She debated briefly whether to stop and pack, then, deciding to do it *after* she'd told him her decision, she braced herself and went back to his bedroom, where she was greeted by the appetizing aroma of freshly brewed coffee.

A heated container, and a low table set with plates, cutlery, napkins, and everything necessary, had been assembled in front of the fire.

Thrown by the intimacy of the little scene, she wished she had stayed safely in her own room. But if Michael had followed through with his half-threat to come and fetch her, it might possibly have made things even more difficult.

Looking elegant in well-cut stone-coloured trousers and a fine black polo-necked sweater, he was pouring coffee.

Glancing up, he said quizzically, 'Just made it. Now come and sit down and tell me if you prefer honey or maple syrup.'

From the container he produced a plate of golden, delicious-looking pancakes.

She had intended to tell him straight away that she was leaving, but instead she found herself saying, 'Maple syrup, please.'

As she prepared to spread the syrup over one of the pancakes firelight glinted on the gold ring she wore on her right hand.

He had noticed the ring previously, but, his attention focused on other things, he had never really *looked* at it.

Now, suddenly, his interest roused, he found himself staring at the engraving, *recognizing* it.

His voice studiedly casual, he remarked, 'That's a most unusual ring.'

When, scarcely listening, mentally rehearsing how to break the news that she was leaving, she said nothing, he pressed, 'How long have you had it?'

'Sorry?'

'The ring you're wearing… How long have you had it?'

'Since I was eighteen.'

'May I ask where it came from?'

'It belonged to my great-grandmother.'

Noting her abstraction, and thinking it best, he dropped the subject for the time being.

The pancakes were every bit as delicious as they looked, and Jenny and her companion who, head bent, appeared to be deep in thought, cleared the plate and emptied the coffee pot while she tried to pluck up the courage to tell him what she had decided.

Breakfast over, and left with no further excuse for delay, she took a deep breath and blurted out, 'This isn't going to work.'

Jolted out of his reverie, he looked up.

Seeing she had his attention, she repeated desperately, 'This isn't going to work.'

He knew at once what she meant, and his heart sank. Clearly she was having second thoughts, regretting what had happened between them. And really he should have known there was a chance that that might happen.

Cursing the impulse that had made him rush her into his bed the previous night, he wished he had taken things more slowly.

Usually he was a great deal more sophisticated, more focused, more laid-back and in control of his actions. He'd always been able to hold back, to wait for something he really wanted.

But somehow Jenny had got under his guard, and he was having difficulty thinking straight and applying his usual self-control.

It was a moment or two before, pretending ignorance, he was able to ask evenly, 'What isn't going to work?'

'This…' She spread helpless palms. 'This whole thing… It should never have happened.'

'You mean sharing my bed?'

'Yes.' Feeling her colour rise, she went on, 'I've never done this kind of thing before. One-night stands and casual affairs aren't for me…'

He was inclined to believe her, which made him wonder

just *why* she had responded to him so ardently. As though following his train of thought, she added jerkily, 'Nor is sleeping with my boss.'

'So you mean you won't be sleeping with me again?'

'No…'

He raised a dark brow.

Vexed with herself, she said sharply, 'I mean I want to leave.'

There was no way he could let her go.

Apart from wanting her in his life, the fact that she had known Slinterwood, taken in conjunction with the ring she was wearing, made him certain that she had some, as yet unexplained, connection with the house and the island.

Unwilling to show his hand until he had more to go on, he tried to settle on the best strategy to employ to keep her here.

Unable to decide, he said lightly, 'I thought you wanted to see how a book comes to life, to help in its creation.'

'I did,' she admitted, 'but now I think it would be best to go.'

'Why?'

'In the circumstances I really can't stay.'

'I don't see why not. If you don't want to share my bed, don't. It isn't compulsory.'

But she *did* want to share his bed, that was the trouble. He drew her, so that she was like the moon held by the earth's gravitational pull.

'If you would prefer to, we can forget everything that's happened between us,' he was going on mendaciously, 'and carry on simply as employer and employee.'

How could she possibly forget what had happened? The memory would always loom between them, insoluble and embarrassing.

At least on her part.

But while it had been life-changing for her, clearly it had meant so little to him that, in order to keep an employee he needed, he was willing to brush it aside and forget it.

Which flayed her pride, making it even more impossible to stay.

She shook her head, and, taking a deep, steadying breath, said, 'If you could just take me across the causeway, I can find my own way back to London.'

If Michael refused to take her, she decided desperately, she would have to find some other means of getting over to the mainland.

However, he was too clever a tactician to precipitate matters by giving an out and out refusal. His tone eminently reasonable, he said, 'Look, don't decide this instant. Leave it until tomorrow and see how you feel then.'

She had opened her mouth to protest, when he added, 'For one thing, it would be highly dangerous to try to cross the causeway in this weather. By tomorrow the storm should have blown itself out, and if you *still* want to go back to London, I'll take you.

'In the meantime, twenty-four hours will give me a chance to try and line up a replacement PA.'

A sense of justice pointed out that she owed him that much. After all, she had agreed to take the job, and she couldn't deny that she was as much to blame for what had happened between them as he was.

Watching her hesitate, he added persuasively, 'If you stay at least for today it will give me an opportunity to show you round the castle.'

Much as she wanted to see the castle, she recognized the offer as bait. Finding her voice, she pointed out, 'But it's raining heavily.'

'Which for the moment rather rules out the battlements. But you could still see the inside.'

'The *inside?*' She felt a quick thrill of excitement. 'Could I really?' Then doubtfully, 'Are you sure the owner won't mind?'

'Quite sure.' He spoke with certainty.

Even so, she knew she ought to refuse. But it seemed a terrible shame to throw away such a chance.

Reading her expression right, and suddenly more confident of success, he added lightly, teasingly, 'And just to set your mind at rest, I promise I won't do anything you don't want me to do.'

Recognizing that confidence, and fairly sure he was laughing at her, she gritted her teeth.

Of course she *could* shatter his assurance and have the last laugh by insisting on leaving the island immediately.

Only she was abruptly convinced that it would be a waste of time. He held the whiphand, and the gleam in his green eyes told her he knew it.

No matter how reasonable he might *appear,* if it came to the crunch she would get no help from him, and the sound of the storm raging outside emphasized the folly of attempting to walk.

Recognizing thankfully that for the moment her opposition was at an end, and promising himself that from now on he would take the softly-softly approach, he said briskly, 'So that's decided. Now I've a quick phone call to make…'

Presumably the phone call would be to an employment agency, in the hope of finding himself a new PA.

'So if you'd like to fetch a mac, I'll meet you downstairs in a few minutes.'

She rose to her feet, and, her legs feeling oddly shaky, went to do as he'd suggested.

Once again her feelings were in turmoil. Mingling with a host of misgivings was a swift and fierce gladness that she wasn't going just yet.

Because of the weather, she had one more day on her island. One more day with Michael. She would forget her embarrassment, forget all her doubts, and do her best to enjoy it.

By the time she had washed her hands, belted a stone-coloured mac around her slender waist, and made her way down to the hall, he was standing waiting by the front door.

He had pulled the car in as close as possible, but even so by the time he had helped her into the passenger seat the shoulders of his short jacket were spattered with rain and his ruffled dark hair was dewed with drops.

A strong wind was buffeting the treetops into a frenzy of activity, and heavy storm clouds were being driven across the sky like a straggling flock of grey ragged sheep.

As they climbed towards the road, through the water that streamed down the windows she could see that the sea was a boiling mass of white-topped breakers.

From being a small child she had loved, and been in tune with, all aspects of the elements. Now something inside responded to the wildness of the weather and, her heart lifting, she wanted to laugh aloud.

As though he sensed and shared her feelings, Michael turned his head to smile at her.

The short drive along the coastal road was quite spectacular, and when they surmounted the ridge Jenny caught her breath at the sight of the castle, bleak and imposing against the stormy sky.

Looking at it, she found herself quoting, '"Four grey walls and four grey towers…"'

Slanting her a glance, Michael offered, 'But not too many flowers at this time of the year.'

She was still marvelling how quickly he'd picked up that spur-of-the-moment quotation when he added, 'I see you know your Tennyson.'

'After we did "The Lady of Shalott" at school he became a firm favourite of mine.'

'Mine too.'

'You like poetry?'

'Yes.'

She was surprised that so masculine a man should admit to enjoying poetry.

Seeming to read her mind, he asked, 'Why not? As a writer I love language in all its forms.'

'Of course. Have you always liked poetry?'

Driving through the castle gatehouse and beneath the port-cullis, he answered, 'Since reading my first nursery rhyme at the age of three, and progressing to Marvell and Donne, it's been only too easy to get drunk on words.'

Words were the tools of his trade, she realized, so it made perfect sense.

Close at hand, the castle looked even more stark and dramatic, with its rain-drenched cobbled courtyard and its high stone walls running in water.

As they drew up close to a huge, iron-studded door Michael remarked slyly, 'I've always rather liked Andrew Marvell's, "To His Coy Mistress".'

Watching the colour mount in her cheeks, he added, 'I see you know it.'

Then instantly contrite, he grimaced. 'Sorry, I shouldn't tease you. But you blush so beautifully that I couldn't resist it.'

He touched her cheek. 'Forgive me?'

The look on his face made him irresistible, and her heart turned over.

'There's nothing to forgive,' she said huskily.

'A truly generous woman,' he commented with a smile. Then, taking a large key from his pocket, he instructed, 'Wait here.'

Having turned the key in the ornate iron lock, he hurried back through the deluge and held the car door against the strong gusts while she clambered out.

In the two or three seconds it took to get inside, the wind and rain beat into her face, almost stopping her breath and blowing loose strands of hair into wild disorder.

Closing the door behind them, Michael said, 'Phew!'

Strangely exhilarated, she raised a glowing face and smiled

at him as she began to peel the stray tendrils of wet hair from her cheeks and tuck them back into the coil as best she could.

Thinking he'd never seen anyone more beautiful, he produced a spotless hankie and, shaking out the folds, used it to dry her face.

Her heart doing strange things and her smile dying away, Jenny stood rooted to the spot looking up at him, her lovely brown eyes wide and defenceless.

The urge to take her in his arms and cover her mouth with his was so strong it was like a physical pain, and he was forced to step back and remind himself firmly of the softly-softly strategy he had decided on.

Jenny had been convinced he was about to kiss her, and when he stepped back she sighed with what she told herself was relief.

But somehow it felt more like regret.

Though she knew, and admitted, it was the road to no-where, she had *wanted* him to kiss her.

Once again she had demonstrated just how dangerous it was to be near him, and if she was to retain any remaining pride or self-respect she must leave as soon as the weather would allow.

As he returned the damp square of cotton to his pocket, and smoothed back his wind-ruffled hair, Jenny took a deep, steadying breath, and transferred her attention to her surroundings.

They were standing in a huge, panelled hall, with a massive stone fireplace and a great oak staircase that climbed to a second-floor landing and a minstrels' gallery.

Picturing the hall with a blazing fire, the metal chandeliers lit with dozens of candles, a colourful throng of people, and the long table groaning with food and drink, she knew that in its heyday it must have been a magnificent sight.

But now, in the flickering grey light that filtered through long, leaded windows awash with water, it looked bare and bleak and deserted.

Even so, she felt a warmth, the same sense of belonging, of coming home, she had felt on seeing Slinterwood for the first time.

Despite that aura of welcoming warmth, the air itself was cold and dank, and as though in response to the realization she shivered.

Noticing that involuntary movement, Michael said crisply, 'There's been no form of heating in this part of the castle for donkey's years, so I suggest we get moving.

'How much of the place do you want to see?'

'I'd like to see it all,' she said, her eagerness and excitement returning with a bound. 'That is, if you don't mind?'

Secretly pleased by her enthusiasm, he said, 'I certainly don't mind, but if you get bored you'll have to tell me.'

How could she get bored when she would be seeing the place she had wanted to see for as long as she could remember, the castle of her dreams?

'I won't get bored,' she said with certainty.

He led the way across the hall and through a door at the end. 'This is the east wing. Neither this, nor the north wing, have been lived in since the early eighteen hundreds, and are empty apart from a few chests and settles and the odd four-poster bed.'

But, for Jenny, even the virtually empty rooms they walked through held an endless fascination, and she looked around her with unflagging interest.

When they reached the end of the north wing, Michael said, 'Beneath here are the dungeons. They're pretty grim-looking, but there's no record of anyone ever having died there.'

From the dungeons they made their way through archways and bare stone passages to the sculleries, kitchens, and store-rooms, the servants' quarters and the servants' hall.

Then, having shown her the gatehouse, which had once been used to house soldiers, the towers, with their arrow-slits and spiral stairways and, above the family vault, the beautiful little chapel—which he told her was still used on special occasions—they returned via backstairs dimly lit by cobwebby windows to the main hall.

As they approached a door near the huge fireplace, above the mantel, she noticed a shield with a familiar design, a phoenix rising from the ashes.

She turned to ask Michael about it, but he was going on, 'And through here is the west wing. It was occupied until the late eighteen hundreds, so the rooms are still fully furnished.'

He led her through a grand living-room, an elaborate music room, a dining-room, a library, and then a magnificent long gallery.

The gallery was elegantly proportioned, with deep, leaded windows made of uneven panes of pale-greenish glass, down which rain streamed incessantly, making the light dim and wavering and giving the place an eerie, under-water feeling.

'It's absolutely beautiful,' Jenny remarked.

'It's said to be haunted.'

'Haunted? By whom?'

He found himself smiling at the excitement in her voice. 'By a lady named Eleanor.'

'Why does she haunt the gallery?'

Lowering his voice to sepulchral tones, he said, 'It's a gory tale of love and hate and jealousy. Sure you want to hear it?'

'Quite sure,' she said.

CHAPTER SEVEN

SMILING at the eagerness in Jenny's voice, Michael began, 'When Lady Eleanor Grey was just eighteen, she fell in love with, and married, Sir Richard D'Envier and came to live at Mirren.

'For a few months they were extremely happy, but Charles, Sir Richard's younger brother, had also fallen in love with Eleanor, and each day he grew more bitterly jealous.

'Eventually, unable to stand it any longer, he hired a couple of cutthroats to waylay Sir Richard and kill him.

'But Richard, a courageous man, fought them off, and, though he was badly wounded, he managed to remount his horse and ride back to the castle, where he died in his wife's arms.

'They were perilous times, and because Eleanor was pregnant she was particularly vulnerable.

'As was the custom in those days, Charles, now head of the household, offered her and her unborn child his protection, if she would marry him.

'Still mourning her husband, Eleanor didn't want to marry again, but for the sake of her unborn child, she felt forced to seriously consider his proposal.

'What she didn't know was that one night after too much wine Charles had boasted that if the child was a boy, he would find some way of getting rid of it.'

Jenny, who had been listening with bated breath, urged, 'Go on.'

'Though Eleanor had never liked her husband's brother, she had almost decided that she had little choice but to accept his proposal when something happened to change her mind.

'Charles had made one serious mistake. Because he believed his ruffians had bungled the murder, he refused to pay them.

'One night, in their cups, the pair aired their grievances, and the news got back to Eleanor. Her dislike of Charles turned into a fierce hatred, and a strong desire for revenge.

'Unaware that she knew the truth, Charles was pressing her for an answer to his proposal, but she bided her time while she thought up a plan to get him away from the retinue that invariably surrounded him.

'Eleanor often walked in the long gallery, and one evening she sent Charles a flirtatious little note saying that if he met her here, she would give him her answer.

'He came, all smiles, and prepared to embrace her. He didn't see the jewelled dagger hidden in the folds of her gown until she plunged it into his heart.

'A bloody and melodramatic tale,' Michael added in his normal voice.

'Did she kill herself too?'

'No. Apparently she had half intended to, but the thought of her unborn child held her back. Luckily for her, there were many at the castle who were still loyal to Sir Richard, and when Charles was hastily buried, and the news spread that he had died of a fever, no one challenged the story.'

'So what happened to Eleanor?'

'Having given birth to a healthy son, whom she named Richard, she survived to see him grow into a fine young man, the image of his father.

'She lived to be forty-five, without ever remarrying, and

according to legend she still walks in the long gallery where she avenged the death of her husband.'

Jenny sighed. 'I'm pleased there's a happy ending after all.'

His smile just a little mocking, Michael asked, 'Don't you feel a spot of womanly pity for poor lovelorn Charles?'

'Certainly not,' she denied crisply. 'He only got what he richly deserved.'

Laughing at her honest indignation, Michael led her up to the top floor, with its dressing-rooms, retiring-rooms and magnificent bedchambers.

When she remarked on the fact that the rooms led straight into one another, he told her, 'At that time there were no upstairs corridors, which must have meant a distinct lack of privacy for any guests. Though they did manage to keep the servants well out of sight.'

'How did they do that?' she asked curiously.

'I'll show you.'

Crossing to one of the inner walls, he moved aside a hanging tapestry to reveal a small door.

'Where possible, the staircases and corridors used by the servants were built between the main walls, and the doors into the various rooms hidden behind hanging tapestries. That way a servant could slip in to make up the fire, and disappear again without being noticed.

'And, speaking of things being hidden, there's a secret passage I haven't yet shown you.'

'A secret passage?'

Jenny, who had been fascinated by the architecture of the old place, the archways and steps that seemed to lead nowhere, the huge fireplaces and the beautiful old windows, gave a shiver of excitement.

Misreading that shiver, he said, 'You're cold.'

She was, frozen through, but she'd been far too engrossed to heed the cold.

'Come on, let's get going.'

Thinking he intended to leave, she protested, 'I'd love to see the secret passage.'

'And so you shall.'

Taking her hand, he hurried her down the stairs and across the hall, and, coming to a halt on the far side of the fireplace, ran his fingers along the oak panelling just above head height.

There was a muffled click, and with a grating noise a section of the panelling moved to one side.

Peering excitedly into the cobwebby gloom, Jenny asked, 'Where does it lead?'

'The first short section leads to the south wing, which is where we're heading, and the second, much longer section, to an escape tunnel which goes down under the walls, through a gap in the rock, and eventually comes out about a quarter of a mile away.'

'Have you ever been through?'

'Oh, yes.'

'I've never been through a secret passage,' she told him. Then hopefully, 'If we're heading for the south wing, do you think we could go that way?'

Quizzically, he charged, 'You've been reading too much Enid Blyton.'

With a grin, she admitted, 'As a child, I loved her books... So could we?'

Amused, he agreed, 'We could. But it will be dark and rough underfoot, and all I have with me is a small pencil-torch.'

'I'm sure we'd manage,' she told him eagerly.

'What if I can't locate the lever that opens the panel to let us out?'

Looking anything but concerned, she suggested, 'Well, if you can't, so long as you leave this panel open we could always retrace our steps.'

'Very well. You'd better follow me.'

As they stepped through the gap, reminding her to tread carefully, he took her hand.

Feeling a delicious thrill of adventure, she followed close on his heels.

The tunnel was narrow, the air cold and musty, the ground uneven beneath their feet.

As they moved away from the open panel, the torch a small spotlight in the surrounding darkness, the walls seemed to close in claustrophobically.

Unconsciously, she gripped his hand tighter.

'Do you want to turn back?'

His voice sounded strangely hollow, disembodied, but the fingers curled round hers were strong and reassuring, and she answered, 'No, no, I'm quite happy, really.'

Once or twice she stumbled, and he asked, 'Okay?'

Each time she answered, 'Fine, thank you.'

After what seemed an age, he said, 'If I remember rightly, we should be just about there.'

As they slowed to a halt he let go of her hand to release the lever. At the same instant she stepped on a loose piece of rubble, and gave a gasp as her left ankle turned painfully.

'What's wrong?' he asked.

'I've twisted my ankle,' she admitted ruefully.

He thrust the torch into his pocket, and his arms went around her.

Standing on one leg, storklike, she leaned against him, grateful for his support.

He could feel the slender weight of her body, smell the apple-blossom scent of her hair and the fragrance of her skin.

She heard the breath hiss through his teeth then, in the darkness, his mouth found hers unerringly, and he was kissing her with a passion that swept her completely away.

How long they stood in the darkness kissing, Jenny never knew. She was in a blissful world of her own, everything else obliterated, forgotten, the touch of his lips and the feel of his arms all she had ever wanted or needed.

Overwhelmed with tenderness, she touched his cheek.

Even against the coldness of his face, he was aware that her fingers felt icy.

The realization waking him to practicalities, he lifted his head, and, one arm still supporting her, felt for the lever.

After a second or two, he found and depressed it, and with a grating sound the panel slid aside, letting in light.

'Can you walk?' he asked.

'Yes, I think—' The words ended in a little cry of pain as she tried to put her weight on her injured left ankle.

Unable to lift her in the narrow space, he ordered tersely, 'Stay where you are and keep that foot off the floor.'

Poised on one leg, one arm braced against the wall, she muttered, 'This is ridiculous.'

'If you attempt to walk on it, it'll only make matters worse.'

Seeing the sense of that, she stopped arguing and did as she'd been bidden.

He went through the opening first, then turned, and, stooping, said, 'Put your arms around my neck and duck your head.'

She obeyed, and, one arm encircling her waist, his free hand shielding her head, he helped her clear of the panelling and swung her up into his arms.

They had emerged into what seemed to be a small inner hall, with a row of high internal windows on one side.

In spite of the turmoil caused by that kiss, and being held against his broad chest, she noticed that the air felt appreciably warmer.

He opened the nearest door into a red-carpeted room with dark oak panelling, and carried her over to a leather couch set in front of a stone fireplace, and put her down amidst the cushioned comfort.

She was surprised to see a fire was already laid in the grate and a box of matches lay waiting. To one side of the hearth a large wicker basket was piled high with logs.

As soon as she was settled with her back against a pile of cushions he pulled off her shoes, dropped them by the old-fashioned fender, and stooped to strike a match.

When the kindling flared and caught hold, he rose to his feet and said with satisfaction, 'There, that should soon be burning nicely. Now you stay here and get warm, and I'll be back in a minute.'

He disappeared through a door in the far wall.

Already able to feel the welcome warmth of the fire on her icy feet, Jenny glanced around her curiously. The room seemed to be a combination of living-room and study, its long, arched windows looking out onto a rain-swept inner courtyard.

Michael had told her the castle was no longer inhabited, but, attractively furnished and homely, with books and ornaments and a grandfather clock that chimed melodiously, this room showed every sign of being lived-in.

A silver-framed photograph standing on the nearby bookcase caught her eye. It was of a handsome man with clear-cut features, blue eyes beneath still dark brows, and iron-grey hair. He looked aristocratic, and she found herself wondering if *he* owned Mirren.

All at once she felt distinctly uncomfortable, an intruder, as if the man might walk in at any moment and demand to know what she was doing here.

It was something of a relief when, a short time later, Michael returned. He had discarded his jacket, and was carrying a first aid box under his arm and two steaming mugs.

'Warmer?' he queried.

'Much. I don't really need this now.' She began to wriggle out of her coat.

He put everything down on a low table that stood close by and helped her.

Tossing it over one of the high-backed chairs, he remarked, 'I thought we could do with a hot drink, as soon as I've had a look at that ankle.'

Sitting down on the edge of the couch, he grimaced. 'I'm afraid it's already starting to swell. We'll just have to hope there's nothing broken.'

Though he was as gentle as possible, she winced as his fingers began to probe

After a moment, he announced, 'There doesn't seem to be, thank the Lord.' Taking a can of analgesic spray from the first-aid box, he added, 'But your feet are like ice.'

The fine spray felt colder still.

'There, that should help to curtail the pain and prevent any further swelling.

'However, a bit of support wouldn't be a bad idea...' Producing a crêpe bandage, he bound her ankle neatly and efficiently.

'Thank you,' she said, when he'd finished. 'That's starting to feel better already.'

He handed her one of the mugs, and, taking a seat in a nearby chair, remarked, 'I'm afraid there's no fresh milk, so I hope you don't mind having your coffee black?'

'No, not at all.'

His eyes on her face, he asked, 'So what's wrong?'

'Nothing,' she assured him. 'I'm fine.'

'You're lying,' he said shortly. 'Apart from your ankle, something's bothering you.'

'I just feel I've no right to be here,' she admitted in a rush. 'If the owner should—'

Something about the look on his face stopped her short, and, light suddenly dawning, she said almost accusingly, '*You* own the castle.'

'That's right,' he agreed.

'The island too?'

'Yes.'

'Why didn't—?' She bit her tongue.

'I tell you?' he finished for her.

'I'm sorry,' she said in confusion. 'Of course you had a perfect right to keep it to yourself.'

'How kind of you to say so.'

Though she felt sure the gentle sarcasm wasn't meant to wound, emotionally friable, she flushed, and her eyes filled with unbidden tears.

He rose to his feet, instantly contrite. 'I'm sorry.' Reaching for her hand, he raised it to his lips and kissed it.

His lips felt warm against her palm, and a shiver ran through her.

'Now, why don't you relax and drink your coffee?'

But his touch had ruffled her even more, and he realized it.

Cursing himself for a fool, he released her hand and began to sip his own coffee.

The fire was blazing merrily now, throwing out a circle of heat. After adding some more logs, he queried, 'Feet warmer?'

Her voice a little stilted, she answered, 'Yes, thank you, warm as toast now.'

Then, sounding more like herself, 'In any case it was well worth getting cold for. The castle is absolutely wonderful.'

Pleased and relieved that she wasn't the kind to bear a grudge, he said, 'I'm very glad you think so. I've always loved the old place.'

'Do you know its history?'

'Oh, yes, it's all in the family archives. Following the battle of Hastings, William the Conqueror gave the island, and a large chunk of the surrounding countryside, to Michel D'Envier, a young Norman duke who had helped raise an army to fight alongside him.

'After Michel fell in love with, and married, the daughter of an English nobleman, he started to build the castle, and it's been home to the D'Envier family since it was completed in the early part of the twelfth century.

'Though internally it's been altered a lot over the years, the outer walls and the battlements, the towers and the gatehouse date from then. That's why I've done my best to maintain the place in good order and keep it structurally sound.'

'That can't be easy.'

'It isn't. Luckily I have the money now, but in the past it's been a big drain on the family resources. That's one of the reasons my father, after being approached by the local historical society, decided to open the unoccupied wings to the public.'

Embarrassed to recall her own comments about visitors dropping litter, she wished she had kept her opinions to herself.

'Oh, I see,' she said a shade awkwardly.

'Personally,' Michael went on, 'I never liked the idea, and after my father died and probate was granted, I reversed that decision.'

A gleam of devilment in his green eyes, he added, 'So you see you have me to blame for your disappointment all those years ago.'

Forgetting her embarrassment, and picking up on his mood, she assured him lightly, 'Well, as you've more than made up for it today, I forgive you.'

'How very magnanimous.'

This time she only smiled.

It was still raining hard, and what little light there had been was fading. Beyond the fireglow that enclosed them in their own little cocoon of well-being, the room was growing dusky.

As soon as she had finished her coffee, he put his own empty cup down, switched on a couple of standard lamps, and, resuming his seat, queried, 'Feel any better now?'

'A lot.' She moved her foot experimentally.

He shook his head. 'I meant now you know you're not trespassing do you feel more relaxed, more comfortable about being here?'

'Oh… Yes… Yes…'

'You don't sound at all sure.'

She wasn't. It was much too cosy. Too intimate. Remembering his kiss in the secret tunnel and her own helpless reaction to it, how could she feel relaxed and comfortable? She ought to be heading home to London, well away from temptation.

After a moment, needing to break the lengthening silence, she remarked, 'Though you told me there was no one living at the castle, it looks and feels as if there could well be.'

'My parents lived here until my mother died some six years ago, and my father followed her less than a year later. Soon after his death, all that remained of the staff—three old family retainers, a man, his wife, and daughter—who had worked at the castle all their lives, decided to retire and go to live in one of the cottages on the estate.

'I didn't want this wing to get damp and neglected, so I arranged with Mrs Blair to come in regularly to clean and air the place and make sure the radiators are working properly.'

'It seems strange to talk about radiators in a castle this old.'

'Castles this old tend to be cold, draughty places, and to make it liveable in the entire south wing was refurbished early in the nineteen hundreds, and a generator and a central-heating system installed.

'It's all very old-fashioned now, but it still works, and hopefully should last until I've drawn up plans to have the whole thing modernized.'

'Why don't you—?' She stopped short.

His eyes on her face, he urged, 'Feel free to ask anything you want to know.'

Encouraged by his words, but determined to be cautious all the same, she admitted, 'I was wondering why, when you come to the island, you don't live here? Or perhaps you do, sometimes?'

He shook his head. 'I used to visit often when my father was alive, and when I'm on the island I still come to spend a day or two and sometimes the odd night here. There's one bed always kept aired. But I haven't actually lived at the castle since I left to go to university. If I'd returned to Mirren after graduating, I would probably have followed the family tradition and taken up residence at Slinterwood.

'You see it was originally intended to be the home of the family's eldest son, that is, until his father died. Then, if his mother was still alive, *she* would move into Slinterwood, while he and his family were expected to take over the castle.'

'So you're the eldest son?'

'I'm the only son.'

Fascinated by what he was telling her, and forgetting her earlier resolve to be cautious, she said, 'But you didn't take over the castle when your father died?'

'No, the circumstances weren't right. I was unmarried and living in London, still trying to find my feet as a writer. However, I decided that one day, if my wife was willing, I *would* move back, as my father had always hoped.'

His voice flat, dispassionate, he added, 'But when I did eventually get married, after coming here on a couple of occasions Claire decided that she hated the island.'

So even if he and his ex-wife did get back together, the castle wouldn't be lived in...

As the silence stretched, knowing that he must be thinking much the same, Jenny made an effort to change the subject.

Indicating the photograph she'd noticed previously, she asked, 'Who's that?'

'My father. I took that picture of him when he was about sixty.'

'A nice-looking man,' she commented. Adding, 'Though your eyes are a different colour, I can see the likeness now.'

'All the D'Envier males seem to have dark hair and that kind of bone structure.'

Which meant that if he ever had children, his sons would probably look like him…

Sighing a little, she pictured two small boys with Michael's clear-cut features, cleft chin, and thick dark hair.

Watching her face grow soft, he wondered what she was thinking.

Since that impulsive kiss in the darkness of the secret passage, his mind had been only partly on what was being said, his concentration seduced by memories of her response. How willingly her cold lips had parted beneath his, how pliantly her body had moulded itself against his body, how eagerly her arms had welcomed him and held him close…

Jenny looked up suddenly, a question trembling on her lips, and their eyes met.

She saw the darkness in his, darkness that held a fierce flame of desire in its depths, and, shaken rigid by that look, and her own response to it, she glanced hastily away.

A log settled in the grate with a rustle and a spurt of orange sparks, and the grandfather clock ticked away the seconds.

'You were about to ask me something?'

Michael's tone held no trace of any emotion other than a kind of casual friendliness, and just for an instant she wondered if she could have imagined that blazing look.

But she knew she hadn't. The memory of it was burnt indelibly into her brain.

Afraid to look at him, she fumbled around for the question that had been on the tip of her tongue.

'I presume, from what you were saying, that the name D'Envier has been anglicized?'

'Yes. My father decided it was time to become totally English, to drop the apostrophe and change the spelling.

'But enough of me and my family. Tell me about yourself

and *your* family. You told me you were born in London and went to live at Kelsay when you were quite young?'

'Yes…'

'Why?'

'My father left when I was two years old, and as my grandparents had been killed in a car crash the previous year my mother took me to live with my great-grandmother.'

'Go on.'

'I really liked living at the seaside, and I loved Gran dearly. Possibly because I was named after her, we seemed to share a special bond.

'But when I was seven, my mother remarried, and took me to live in the Channel Islands. I was very sad to have to leave Gran. I missed her a lot. We stayed in Jersey for nine years, then my parents decided to move to France.

'I'd never got on particularly well with my stepfather, so I chose to go back to Kelsay and live with Gran. By this time she was very old and frail and had recently suffered a stroke. So for the next two years, while I finished my schooling, I helped to look after her…'

Though she had talked, obediently following his lead, right from the start part of her mind had been taken up by her companion.

Or rather by her *awareness* of him.

Though she avoided looking at him, she was conscious of every single thing: his light breathing, the slight rise and fall of his chest, the movement of his hands, the flick of his dark lashes when he blinked, and the faint, masculine scent of his aftershave. She was even convinced she could hear the beat of his heart.

'You mentioned that the ring you're wearing had belonged to your great-grandmother?'

'Yes.'

Reaching across the table he took her hand, and twisting the ring between his finger and thumb, remarked, 'A beautiful old signet ring like this is bound to have a fascinating history. What exactly do you know about it?'

Her heart lurching drunkenly at his touch, she half shook her head. 'Well, nothing, really…'

Sounding a little breathless, she added, 'I know Gran always wore it. I recall seeing it on her finger when I was quite small.'

Making a determined effort, she withdrew her hand, and went on, 'When I went back to nurse her, she was still wearing it. I would have liked to have asked her where it came from, but the stroke, as well as leaving her partially paralyzed, had made her practically unintelligible, and trying to talk upset her.'

'So after her death you inherited the ring?'

'Not exactly. The night she died I was sitting with her. In the early hours of the morning, she awakened from a doze. Seeing I was there, she pulled the ring off her finger, and pressed it into my hand.

'She tried very hard to tell me something, but the words were garbled. To save her any further distress, I pretended to understand. I put the ring on my own finger, and promised to always wear it. Then I laid her hand on top of it, sandwiched between my own two hands…'

Michael got a vivid mental picture of a very old wrinkled hand, held lovingly between two young, strong hands, and felt a lump in his throat.

'She gave a little, contented sigh, and a short time later slipped peacefully away. I wish she *had* been able to tell me what she so obviously wanted to tell me. If there really is a story attached to the ring, I would have liked to have heard it.'

'Presumably you know what the engraving is?'

'Oh, yes, it's a phoenix. I noticed several as we walked round the castle, and there's a similar one carved on the mantel in the library at Slinterwood. I believe in the past mythical birds and beasts were often used for ornamentation.'

'You're quite right. And of course they were frequently

used in heraldry, and sometimes to illuminate manuscripts and old family trees.'

'Such as yours, presumably?'

'Yes.' Casually, he added, 'One day I'll show you.'

But she wouldn't be here 'one day'. The thought was like a physical pain.

Watching her face, noting the spasm that crossed it, and guessing the cause, he decided the time had come to dig a little deeper.

'How much do you know about your ancestry?' he asked evenly.

'Not a great deal. I really can't go very far back at all.'

'Then start with your great-grandmother. Where was she born and bred?'

'To the best of my knowledge Gran was born in Kelsay and lived there all her life.'

'Tell me about her.'

Knowing it was safer to keep talking, she went on, 'Gran was a lovely person, warm-hearted and generous, with a sense of humour and a belief in the goodness of life that somehow managed to survive losing the one man she really loved…'

His interest quickening, Michael asked, 'How did that happen?'

'When she was only eighteen she fell deeply in love and got engaged to be married. But, tragically, her fiancé died.'

'Do you know his name, or where he came from?'

'I'm afraid not. The only thing I recall my mother telling me was that he was a widower with a young son, and about ten years older than Gran. But apparently they had adored each other and she mourned him for years…'

With an effort, Michael bit back his excitement. What Jenny had just told him had made a nebulous idea that had been forming at the back of his mind crystallize into something like a certainty.

All he needed now was proof. And he thought he knew exactly where to find it, but that would have to wait until the next day.

Bringing his mind back to the present, he said, 'But presumably she married sooner or later?'

'Oh, yes... Eventually she met and married a man named Charles Peacock, and Margaret, my grandmother, was born three years later.'

'Go on.'

'Margaret married George Rider, and had my mother, whose name is Louise. When my mother was twenty-two she married my father, Jonathan Mansell, and I was born a couple of years later.

'I'd never really thought about it before,' she added, 'but it seems strange that for the past three generations only single girls have been born.

'I know my mother would have liked another child, but my stepfather, who had two children by a previous marriage, didn't want any more.'

'What about you?' Michael asked. 'Do you intend to have children?'

The question took her by the throat. Swallowing hard, she answered jerkily, 'I'd always hoped to...'

She stopped speaking as, outside in the darkness, a fierce squall of wind and rain battered against the windowpanes.

'It still sounds rough out there,' Michael remarked. Adding, after a moment, 'The coastal road can be tricky in the dark and in this kind of weather, so I think it might make a lot of sense to stay here for the night.'

CHAPTER EIGHT

'STAY here?' Jenny's voice sounded high and panicky.

'Why not? After all, there's nothing really to go back for. Though there's no fresh food, there's plenty to eat in the store cupboard, so we won't starve by any means.'

'I'm sure food's not a problem, but…'

Her apprehension was palpable, and hovered between them like a chaperon.

Michael glanced at her from beneath long, thick lashes. 'You're worried about the sleeping arrangements?'

'You said there was *one* bed kept aired.'

'Which of course you can have, if you prefer. But I was going to suggest that you might like to sleep in front of the fire?

'You see, the couch you're on is a bed-settee. To the best of my knowledge it's nice and comfortable, and should be a great deal cosier than the bedroom.'

Jenny thought quickly. Because of her damaged ankle, staying here might prove to be the lesser of two evils.

If they went back to Slinterwood, apart from getting to and from the car there would be stairs to climb, and Michael might insist on carrying her.

Just the idea of being carried up to bed in his arms sent a quiver through her.

'So what do you think?'

She swallowed, then said, 'I'm quite happy to stay here tonight, so long as tomorrow morning I can be back at Slinterwood in good time to pack.'

He sighed. So she was still bent on leaving.

'Well, if that's what you really want,' he agreed evenly. 'But I was rather hoping you might have changed your mind.'

Trying to sound cool and decided, she said, 'No, I haven't changed my mind.'

In spite of all her efforts, Michael heard the quiver in her voice, and, knowing she was nowhere near as unmoved as she was endeavouring to make out, smiled to himself.

'Well, in that case,' he said smoothly, 'I think, as we only had a light brunch, it might be a good idea to eat before too long, then we can get an early night. Don't you agree?'

She had been prepared for him to argue, and, both surprised and relieved that he had put up no further opposition, she nodded.

'Let me know when you're starting to feel hungry.'

Eager to get the evening over, she told him, 'I'm ready to eat whenever you are.'

'Then I'll go and see what I can rustle up.'

'Do you need any help?'

He shook his head. 'We have the remains of a hamper from Fortnum and Mason, so I should be able to manage a meal of some kind.

'There's a dining-room next door,' he added, 'but in the circumstances it might be better to eat on our knees in front of the fire.'

'That suits me fine,' she agreed.

Rising leisurely to his feet, he tossed some more logs onto the fire, sending a shower of bright sparks crackling up the chimney, and, having collected the coffee mugs, went through to the kitchen.

While he was sorting through the cupboard and assembling a meal of sorts, his thoughts were even busier than his hands.

Though with so many unanswered questions, so much at stake, he had absolutely no intention of letting Jenny leave at this stage in the game, he knew it would pay to tread carefully.

To start with, he warned himself, he must hide his desire for her. He had seen how very uncomfortable any sign of its existence made her.

He was practically sure of three things, however.

Firstly, that she wanted *him* as much as he wanted *her.* All her actions seemed to prove it.

Secondly, that her discomfort was almost certainly due to the fact that it went against both her nature and her convictions to indulge in what she regarded as casual sex.

And thirdly, that even though she felt it was completely wrong to sleep with her boss, she couldn't trust herself to hold out against him.

The latter conclusion caused a storm of feeling and a surge of sexual excitement that he had to struggle hard to stifle.

At first, his distrust of the female sex had made him try to ignore an attraction he had told himself was purely physical.

But he no longer believed that that was all it was. What he felt for Jenny, while he hesitated to put a name to it, went a great deal deeper. Somehow it had quietly taken over and become a force to be reckoned with, a fever in his blood.

His thoughts turning to the coming night, and recalling her warmth, her sweetness, her innocent passion, he felt a strong urge to throw caution to the winds and make her his once more.

But was that passion as innocent as it seemed? Suddenly recalling what Paul had told him, he found himself wondering if perhaps there might be some truth in the rumours.

No, he couldn't believe it.

Or was it simply that he didn't *want* to believe it?

Though not much time had passed, knowing Paul never let the grass grow under his feet, and in need of some kind of reassurance, he took his phone out of his coat pocket and rang Paul's mobile.

When there was no answer, he left a cautious message asking if there were any results yet from 'the enquiry'.

He was just about to drop the phone into his trouser pocket when it buzzed.

'That was quick,' he said. 'So where were you?'

'I don't know who you were expecting to call,' Claire's clear, light voice said, 'but I don't suppose it was me.'

'No, it wasn't,' he told her flatly.

'You don't sound very pleased to hear from me,' she said plaintively.

Ignoring that, he asked, 'Why are you calling?'

'I wanted to talk to you.'

'We've nothing left to talk about.'

'But of course we have. The press seem to believe that we're getting back together.'

'Could that be because you told them we were?'

'Darling, don't sound so cross. I only mentioned it as a possibility. I still love you, and I miss you so. I didn't realize just how much I loved you until it was too late.

'Look, suppose I came to see you? We could discuss things, sort out exactly where we stand—'

'My dear Claire, I already know exactly where *I* stand. As far as I'm concerned our marriage is over. Finished. Nothing you can say or do will alter that—' But Michael was talking to himself.

Slipping the phone into his trouser pocket, he grimaced. He didn't believe for one instant that Claire still loved him; in fact he'd come to the conclusion that she never had.

A career as a photographic model was a notoriously precarious one, and at twenty-six she might soon be replaced by a fresh and dewy seventeen-year-old.

Added to that, her former lover had proved to be fickle and

moved on, so no doubt she was regretting even more the ending of her marriage and the loss of a lifestyle that had been very much to her taste…

In the other room, sitting gazing into the flames, her thoughts on the coming night, Jenny tried to tell herself that there was no need to be worried.

She had little doubt that, as far as it went, Michael would keep his mocking promise not to do anything she didn't want him to do.

But that left her wide open.

And suppose he decided to test her? Suppose he kissed her goodnight?

She could tell him to stop, of course, but he was a sophisticated man, skilful and experienced, a man who might choose to ignore what she *said* and judge solely by her reactions.

If he did, she would be lost, and she knew it.

It was her inability to trust herself to say no, and mean it, that had renewed her determination to leave in the morning.

But first she had to get through tonight…

The door opened and Michael came in wheeling a trolley loaded with food and a bottle of white wine.

Her pulse began to race just at the sight of him.

The sleeves of his black polo-necked sweater were pushed up to his elbows exposing muscular forearms, a chef's apron was tied around his lean waist, and there was a dark smudge on his cheek.

It made his hard face look oddly boyish, and her heart melted like candlewax in a flame.

At that instant, as though becoming aware of it, he raised a hand and rubbed the mark off, before saying, 'I'm afraid it's not exactly what you'd call a *usual* meal, so a nice bottle of Chablis might help it down.'

He put the trolley near to the settee, drew his own chair closer, and reached to open and pour the wine.

She watched his hands, strong, well-shaped hands, with long fingers, and neatly trimmed nails, and a teasingly light touch.

How gently they had stroked and caressed her, how tenderly they had cupped the weight of her breasts and teased the nipples into life, how delicately they had traced the skin of her inner thighs, before going on to explore the slick warmth that awaited…

All at once Michael glanced up, and, feeling the hot blood pour into her face, she stared into the flames.

Looking at her half-averted face he saw that she was as scarlet as a Judas flower and the tip of one small ear glowed red.

When, a moment or two later, she sneaked a glance at him, hoping he would put her high colour down to the heat of the fire, she saw he was smiling a little, as if he knew quite well what erotic thoughts had caused that burning blush. But to her great relief he made no comment.

When he handed her a glass, she took a sip of the cool, smooth wine while he spread a napkin on her knee and helped her to a plateful of food.

The meal, which proved to be surprisingly tasty, was comprised of spicy chicken breasts, tinned asparagus, and artichoke hearts. It was followed by bottled apricots in a creamy brandy sauce.

Apart from the odd remark they ate in a silence that, in spite of both their efforts to lighten the atmosphere, was weighted with sexual tension.

When they had finished eating, Michael stacked their dirty dishes on the trolley and took them through to the kitchen.

He returned quite quickly with a tray of coffee and Benedictine, and thin, gold-wrapped mints.

Her mind had been on other things, and as he unloaded the contents of the tray onto the table Jenny said a somewhat belated, 'Thank you very much for the meal.'

Imagining Claire's reaction had she been presented with

what, in effect, was a scratch meal out of tins, Michael said ruefully, 'I won't ask if you enjoyed it, but at least it should keep the pangs of hunger away until the morning.'

'As a matter of fact I thoroughly enjoyed it.'

She sounded as if she meant it, and, marvelling at her good temper and adaptability, he smiled at her.

Riveted by the warmth of that smile, she sat quite still gazing at him.

Her eyes were soft and luminous, and held a mixture of emotions that he didn't dare try to decipher, but that drew him like a magnet.

As though under a spell of enchantment, he rose to his feet, knowing he simply *had* to kiss her.

He had taken just one step when the spell was broken by the buzz of his mobile phone.

Wishing he'd switched if off, he turned away with a murmured, 'Excuse me.'

Shaken by how near she had come to disaster—if he'd touched her it wouldn't have stopped at kissing, she knew— and still quaking inside, Jenny turned away to stare into the fire once more.

Flicking open the phone, Michael said a curt, 'Hello?'

'Hi.' It was Paul's voice. 'Sorry I missed your call earlier, but I was on my way to Bayswater. As it was a delicate matter, I decided it would be better to handle things myself.

'I began by phoning Miss Mansell's flat and talking to her flatmate, whose name is Laura Fleming. When I told Miss Fleming who I was and mentioned that there were some rather unpleasant rumours being circulated about Miss Mansell, she asked me to go over.

'She turned out to be a pleasant, down-to-earth girl, and while we chatted I discovered that I know her boyfriend, Tom Harmen. We both go to the same leisure centre. In fact on a couple of occasions we've played squash together when our respective partners failed to show up.

'But to get to the point, when I told Miss Fleming what was being said about her flatmate she was both furious and indignant. She knows Miss Mansell well, they've been friends and flatmates for a number of years, and she categorically denied that there was a word of truth in those rumours. In fact she was all for coming into Global and laying into the man responsible for them. But I assured her that now I knew they were lies, I would deal with the culprit myself and make sure that the rumours were scotched.

'So all in all, I think you can rest assured that your new PA is squeaky clean.'

'Thanks,' Michael said, 'I appreciate all the trouble you've gone to.'

'Any time. Now I must dash, I'm taking Joanne out to supper. Take care!'

'And you.'

Michael dropped the phone back into his pocket and resumed his seat.

Jenny, who had been in a brown study, looked up.

Though she had guessed that he intended to kiss her and known she should stop him, she had sat helpless and waiting.

When the phone had distracted him, aware that she should feel relieved, she had felt anything but.

But somehow, for her own sake, she *had* to find a way to conquer this weakness. If she gave in to him tonight, it would be total surrender. She wouldn't have the strength to leave in the morning, and they both knew it.

Then she would become his plaything, his temporary mistress, someone who meant nothing to him apart from a little easy pleasure while he taught his ex-wife a lesson, before taking her back.

No! She couldn't do it. *Wouldn't* do it.

Glancing up, she noticed that he was watching her intently, as though endeavouring to read her thoughts.

It unnerved her, and, needing something to occupy her hands and help to hide her feelings, she reached to pick up the jug of coffee and fill two cups, while Michael opened the Benedictine and poured a measure of the golden liqueur into a pair of brandy glasses.

Sitting in the warmth of the fireglow, they drank their coffee and sipped the sweet liqueur in silence.

But while neither of them spoke, she was only too aware that his eyes seldom left her face.

In the aftermath of the phone call, she had noticed that he seemed to be more relaxed, more certain, as though some private worry had been resolved and he could see his way forward.

Now, his mouth firm, the light of conquest in his eye, he looked like a man who intended to storm the fortress and succeed at all costs.

Feeling the vibes, and sensing that she was the object of his planned siege, she felt shivers begin to chase down her spine.

Telling herself she was being a fanciful idiot, she struggled to dismiss the idea.

As the grandfather clock chimed nine-thirty, he remarked, 'Well, if we are going to have an early night, it's about time I was starting to make up the bed-settee.'

She found herself holding her breath when he rose, and, taking the empty glass from her nerveless fingers, set it down, before moving the table against the far wall.

When he turned back his face was bland, anything but threatening. And as if to prove that she really *had* let her imagination run away with her, he said, 'If you'd like to use the bathroom while I do it, you'll find a robe and plenty of toilet things.'

Glancing down at her bandaged ankle, he added, 'My bedroom has an en-suite, so there's no need to try and hurry.'

He stooped purposefully, and before she could tell him she

didn't need any help he had slid an arm behind her back and one under her knees and lifted her into his arms.

Carrying her through to a bathroom that, though old-fashioned, was warm, well equipped and spotlessly clean, he lowered her carefully onto a cork-topped stool.

Then, opening the door of an airing cupboard, he took out some towels and a pile of bedclothes before asking, 'Will you be able to manage?'

There was a another stool in the shower cubicle, and several handgrips, and she answered hastily, 'Oh, yes, thank you.'

'Well, call if you need me.' He hung the towels over the rail and departed with the bedclothes, leaving her to prepare for the night.

Perched on the stool, she managed to wriggle out of her clothes with relative quickness and ease, but because of the need to manoeuvre to keep her bandage dry it took a lot longer than usual to shower.

When she had finished and dried herself, she stood up carefully, and, taking her weight on her good foot, hopped to the sink.

Amongst an array of toiletries, there were tubes of toothpaste, several plastic-encased toothbrushes, and a hairbrush and comb.

A coffee-coloured satin robe lay folded on a nearby shelf, but, guessing that it must have belonged to his ex-wife, she was reluctant to use it.

Having washed and cleaned her teeth, she brushed out her dark hair, and, leaving it to curl loosely around her shoulders, debated what to sleep in.

The thought of Michael seeing her in her skimpy undies threw her into a tizzy, and she decided she had very little option but to borrow the robe.

She had just belted it around her waist and folded her clothes when there was a tap at the door, and Michael's voice queried, 'Are you about ready?'

'Yes, quite ready, thank you. But I really don't need any help.'

Ignoring that obvious untruth, he came in.

It must have taken her even longer than she had realized, because he was wearing a short silk robe and was clearly fresh from the shower himself.

He carried her through to the living-room where the lamps had been switched off, the fire was burning brightly, and the bed-settee, with its pretty, sprigged duvet and plumped up pillows, looked cosy and inviting.

Settling her back against the soft pillows, he sat down on the edge of the settee and smiled into her eyes.

'Don't!' she begged huskily.

Lifting a dark brow, he asked, 'Don't what?'

'You promised you wouldn't do anything I didn't want you to do.'

'And I have every intention of keeping that promise,' he assured her silkily. 'But I'm quite sure you want me to do this.' Tilting her chin, he kissed her with slow deliberation.

His kiss was so feather-light that he could feel her lips trembling beneath his own.

When she made an effort to draw away, he took her face between his hands, and continued to kiss her, little plucking kisses that coaxed and tantalized and beguiled, yet somehow she managed to keep her lips closed against him.

Instead of forcing the issue, his mouth began to stray over her face, planting soft, baby kisses on her cheeks, the tip of her nose, her closed eyelids, and the smooth skin beneath her jawline.

Feeling the way her pulse was racing, he began to nuzzle her neck, and she started to shudder helplessly as, using his lips and teeth and tongue, he delicately nibbled his way down to the warm hollow at the base of her throat.

When his mouth returned to hers once more, and the tip of his tongue stroked across her lips, they parted beneath his coaxing as if there were no help for it.

Even when he deepened the kiss, it was slow and careful,

as if the gift of her mouth was infinitely precious to him. She had no defences against the sweetness and tenderness of that gentle seduction.

He continued to kiss her, and soon she was drifting in a kind of blissful daze where neither the past nor the future existed, and nothing in the world mattered but this Michael's touch and his kisses.

She was hardly aware that his hands had left her face and his fingers had pushed aside the satin lapels of the gown.

It was only when he bent his dark head to take a velvety nipple in his mouth that, panic-stricken, she jerked into life.

If she didn't stop him now, she was lost.

Twining her fingers in his hair, she tugged.

He drew back, and just for an instant she glimpsed a look on his face that echoed the kind of bliss she had been feeling before that sudden attack of panic.

'What's wrong, my love?'

There was no trace of the anger she had expected, and his quiet endearment made her heart stop.

Dragging the lapels together over her breasts, she said hoarsely, 'I don't want you to make love to me.'

He shook his head. 'All your reactions tell me plainly that you *do* want me to make love to you.'

'I *don't*,' she insisted.

Sounding completely unmoved, he said quietly, 'You're lying.'

Gritting her teeth, she said, 'I told you before, I've never believed in casual sex, and I don't want to get involved with my boss.'

'You're already involved,' he pointed out flatly.

'That was a mistake I'm bitterly sorry for. I only wish it had never happened…'

Just for an instant he looked as if she'd struck him, and her heart turned over.

'For one thing,' she ploughed on desperately, 'there's your wife—'

'My ex-wife,' he corrected. 'And as far as Claire's concerned I'm—'

'Don't tell me,' Jenny broke in bitterly. 'You're in no hurry to take her back until you're satisfied that she's learnt her lesson. Well, I've always believed that if you marry someone you should be faithful to them—'

She stopped abruptly, biting her lip. 'I'm sorry, I shouldn't have said that. It sounds terribly strait-laced and judgmental.'

His expression unreadable, he said, 'That kind of thinking certainly sounds a little old-fashioned in this day and age. However, that isn't to say I think you're wrong…'

He took her hand and held it, his thumb stroking over the palm.

'Though no doubt Claire would. Her attitude has always been a great deal more worldly. She regards the body simply as something to dress up and get pleasure from.

'And if by any chance we *did* remarry, when the honeymoon period was over, I'm sure she would want to revert to a "modern" relationship.'

She snatched her hand free. 'Well, *she* may be happy with that, but I wouldn't want any part of it. I don't intend to end up as a temporary plaything, "a bit on the side".'

'Who said anything about a plaything, or "a bit on the side"?'

Realizing that he wasn't about to take no for an answer, desperate now, and suddenly seeing a way out, she lied unsteadily, 'In any case there's someone else to consider…'

His eyes narrowed to green slits. 'Really? So who else is there, may I ask?'

'Someone who… It doesn't really matter.'

'Oh, but it does.'

She had hoped not to have to say any more, but the intentness of his gaze told her that there wasn't a cat in hell's chance of leaving it like that.

'So who is this *someone?* A secret boyfriend perhaps?'

'Not exactly secret,' she said.

'But a boyfriend you failed to mention?'

'Well, yes.'

'At the interview you led me to believe there was no one of any importance in your life.'

When she said nothing, he pursued, 'So if you expect me to believe in this man's existence you'll have to tell me more about him. To start with, what does he do?'

Pushed into a corner, and thinking of Laura's boyfriend, Tom, she answered, 'He works for one of the smaller airlines.'

'How long have you two been going out together?'

'Quite a while.'

'Is it serious?'

After a momentary hesitation, she said, 'Yes.'

Watching her face closely, and almost certain that she was lying, he queried, 'How serious? He hasn't by any chance produced a ring and proposed?'

'As a matter of fact, he has.'

'So why did you lie to me at the interview?'

'I… I didn't,' she denied.

'You told me you hadn't a fiancé.'

Hoping Laura would forgive her, she said, 'I haven't. I didn't accept his proposal.'

'Why not?'

'I—I needed time to think it over.'

'So you decided to take the job until you'd made up your mind?'

'Yes.'

'Didn't he object to you leaving London?'

'He doesn't know anything about it. He's abroad on

business for the next few weeks, and we agreed not to contact each other while he was away.'

'But presumably he'll be expecting an answer when he gets back?'

'Yes.'

'What do you intend to tell him?'

Deciding to stall, she said, 'I still haven't made up my mind.'

'What's he like?'

'Kind and thoughtful and generous.'

'Describe him.'

A little wildly, she said, 'He's in his early twenties, blond, handsome, fun to be with, and loaded with charm.'

'Every girl's dream,' Michael commented sarcastically. 'You said he was generous. Does that mean he buys you presents?'

Growing increasingly stressed, she said, 'He bought me a gift for St Valentine's day.'

'What kind of a gift?'

'A bracelet watch.'

'I haven't seen you wearing it.'

'It's too dressy for work. It's the kind of thing you'd wear in the evening, or for special occasions.'

'So why weren't you wearing it at Mr Jenkins's retirement party?'

'How do you know I wasn't?' Then almost accusingly, 'You were there!'

'For a short time.'

It gave her a strange feeling to realize that he had been at the party and she hadn't even seen him.

'But it was only for Global's staff and employees,' she protested, 'so how did you—?'

Breaking off, she answered her own question. 'Of course, you're a friend of Paul Levens.'

Then recalling Michael's reputation for being antisocial, she asked, '*Why* were you there?'

'I came especially to have a look at you.'

For a moment she was taken aback, then realization dawned. 'You mean before you asked Mr Levens to set up the interview?'

A gleam in his eye, he asked, 'Can you blame me?'

'No, I suppose not.'

Returning to the attack, he said, 'But we were discussing your boyfriend. Do you and he sleep together?'

'No.'

'Why not?'

Desperate to get the interrogation over, she said, 'Until now I haven't been absolutely sure of my feelings.'

'*Until now*... Does that mean you've finally made up your mind?'

She swallowed, then, knowing she had to sound convincing, said, 'Yes. I love him.'

Momentarily, Michael's certainty that she was lying was rocked.

Then the way she was avoiding his eyes made him wonder, and he returned to the attack once more.

'If you had been sure of your feelings previously, would you have slept with him?'

'I—I might have done.'

'But you would have to love a man before you went to bed with him?'

'Yes.'

'By the way, you still haven't told me what this boyfriend of yours is called.'

Her mind went completely and utterly blank.

Seeing he was waiting, and knowing that everything depended on being able to answer convincingly, she blurted out, 'His name's Tom Harmen. Now I refuse to answer any more questions.'

All uncertainty set at rest, Michael felt a surge of mingled relief and triumph.

'Just one last thing. How do you feel about me?'

'What?'

'I asked how you felt about me? Do you love me?'

'No—no, of course not,' she stammered.

'So why *did* you go to bed with me?'

'I've told you,' she cried jerkily. 'I hadn't intended it to happen.'

'You couldn't help yourself?'

When she failed to answer, just stared at him, he smiled, a slow smile of satisfaction that made her blood run cold, and she heard the clang of the trap closing behind her even before he drew her close and kissed her.

CHAPTER NINE

THOUGH Jenny wanted so badly to stay in Michael's arms, somehow she gathered the will power to pull herself free. 'No. I can't let this happen. I—'

'If you're going to tell me again that you have a boyfriend you love, you're wasting your time. I know you're lying,' he added flatly.

She half shook her head, then said in despair, 'No, that isn't it.'

'So what is?'

'You know perfectly well.'

'Tell me something. If Claire wasn't still in the picture, would you feel the same?'

'But she *is*.'

'That's just it, she isn't. You see—'

'How can you say that? If you think for just one moment that I —'

Putting a finger against her lips to stop the indignant flow of words, Michael said patiently, 'Will you please listen to me? I have absolutely no intention of taking Claire back. Everything was absolutely over, finished, when I divorced her.'

He paused to let that sink in while she stared at him, her lovely brown eyes mirroring her hopes and fears and remaining doubts.

'Over?'

'Over.'

Hardly able to believe it, she whispered, 'You won't be taking her back?'

'No matter what lies she may be feeding to the newspapers, I *won't* be taking her back.'

Then with soft impatience, 'Now will you be still and let me make love to you before this wanting burns me up...?'

He wasn't taking his ex-wife back. *He wasn't taking her back!*

Jenny gave a little sigh, and as he bent his head her eyes drifted shut, and her chin rose to expose the long line of her throat.

Running his fingers into her dark, silky hair, he held her face between his palms and kissed her with a passionate tenderness.

It was all over between them. She heard the angels singing as she kissed him back.

For a while they just kissed. Then kissing was no longer enough, and, having removed her robe, he tossed aside his own and stretched out beside her.

While the fireglow warmed her and gilded her skin, his hands began a slow journey of exploration, caressing every inch of her body, finding all her secret places and making every nerve-ending sing into glorious life.

When his mouth followed his hands, she began to shudder as, whispering how beautiful she was, how much pleasure she gave him, how much he wanted her, he brought her to a fever pitch of desire.

Then he paused, supporting himself on one elbow while he gazed down at her.

Opening dazed eyes, she stared up at him.

There was a strange expression on his face, a look of hope, a kind of expectancy, as if he was waiting for something.

Her heart answered that look, and, smiling at him, she put her arms around his neck and heard his sigh of contentment and pleasure as she pulled him down into the cradle of her hips.

He made love to her in silence—tender, passionate love that needed no words.

Somehow that silence made the other sensations grow stronger, more intense, and while they moved in unison stars seemed to rain down on them like sparks, making them burn with ecstasy.

In the aftermath of their love-making, when she lay limp and quivering, her eyes closed, he drew her into his arms and, knowing beyond a shadow of a doubt that he had made the right decision, *she* was the woman he wanted, held her against his heart until she fell fast asleep.

Then he lay looking down at her lovely, peaceful face— the dark curve of her brows and the long sweep of lashes, the small straight nose and the wide, passionate mouth, the high cheekbones and the firm chin that gave her face so much character—and wondered at that indefinable quality that made a set of features unique and beautiful.

Features that had already been familiar to him the first time he'd set eyes on her.

And suddenly, the knowledge swimming from the depths of his mind, he knew exactly why.

When he eventually slipped into sleep, the final parts of the jigsaw had been fitted together and made a clear and fascinating picture.

Jenny awoke in the morning to instant remembrance and a surging happiness. It was all over between Michael and Claire. He wasn't going to take her back.

Hopes and dreams for the future danced in her mind as bright and entrancing as fireflies, and, smiling a little, she stretched luxuriously.

The grate had been cleared and a fresh fire was burning cheerfully, only to be diminished somewhat by pale winter sunshine slanting through the mullioned windows, its brightness matching her mood.

She had slept cradled in Michael's arms, and earlier he had kissed her awake and made love to her again. Long, slow, delectable love that had left her feeling treasured and beautiful and desirable.

Things she had never felt before. Things that, after Andy, she had never even *hoped* to feel.

And perhaps even more important, he had given her a sense of safety and fulfilment, as though she had at last found her true home in his arms.

But for the moment she was alone, and the smell of percolating coffee was drifting in.

Pushing back the duvet, she sat on the edge of the bed and gingerly tested her ankle.

Finding the night's rest had made all the difference, and though still a trifle painful it took her weight, she unwound the bandage and made her way into the bathroom.

When she had showered, she pulled on her clothes, cleaned her teeth, brushed her hair, and, eager to be with Michael, went through to the kitchen.

It was a pleasant enough room, with a wood-burning stove standing in a stone fireplace, an oak table and chairs, and, though they were somewhat out of date, 'all mod cons'.

There was a glass jug of coffee keeping hot on the stove, along with a dish of something that smelled extremely appetizing, but to her disappointment there was no sign of Michael.

Returning to the living-room, she folded the bedding and left it in a neat pile on the settee, then, favouring her damaged ankle, went exploring.

From the inner hall they had come in by, an archway led to what appeared to be a formal drawing-room, and beyond that a butler's pantry. Further on still was a small oak door, which, when she tried it, opened into the main courtyard.

Outside it seemed reasonably mild, and, deciding that she didn't need a coat, she set off across the cobbles, pausing by the old metal-capped well to look around her at the picturesque scene.

The storm had passed through in the early hours of the morning, giving place to a relatively bright, sunny day.

Everywhere still looked freshly washed. The cobblestones gleamed and a million raindrops glittered on sills and guttering, the bonnet of Michael's car, and the ivy that festooned the southern wall.

She sighed with pleasure.

A seagull circled, calling raucously, and, tilting back her head to follow that beautiful, effortless flight, she noticed a figure on the battlements.

As she looked up their eyes met and held.

She had the strangest feeling of déjà vu.

Only it *wasn't* déjà vu, she realized as she absently watched the seagull settle on the cover of the well, its beady eyes fixed on her, its yellow webbed feet looking clumsy on so graceful a bird; this had really happened.

On her very first visit to the castle, she had looked up and seen a man with dark, wind-ruffled hair standing on the battlements.

Their eyes had met and held, and as though something momentous had happened her breath had caught in her throat and her heart had started to throw itself against her ribs.

Flustered both by the strength of her reaction and the intensity of the man's gaze, she had looked away.

It had been quite late, and, knowing herself to be the only visitor still there, she had wondered if the environs of the castle were closed and she should have been gone.

That thought in mind, she had started across the courtyard

towards the main gate, but something had impelled her to pause just briefly and turn to look up at the battlements once more.

They were empty. The man who had had such an impact on her had vanished.

But the little incident had stayed in her mind for a long time afterwards.

Now she was sure that it had been Michael she had seen all those years ago, and, wondering at the strangeness of fate, she looked up to wave to him.

The battlements were empty. He had vanished once more.

She felt a sense of loss like a blow over the heart, a sudden panic, a fear that history was repeating itself.

Then, just as the seagull took to the air with a squawk, Michael's tall figure appeared from the north tower and started to cross the courtyard towards her.

Filled with gladness, she literally threw herself into his arms.

He gave a little grunt as he took the unexpected impact, and held her close.

When she'd been thoroughly kissed, a twinkle in his eye, he told her gravely, 'Now that's what I call real enthusiasm.'

Blushing a little, she murmured, 'Sorry.'

'There's no need to be sorry. I only hope I can look forward to a greeting like that every morning. I just couldn't help but wonder what brought it on.'

'I know it sounds silly, but I thought for a minute that you'd gone.'

'Gone?' he echoed blankly.

'Disappeared… Like you did the first time. You see, when I looked up and saw you standing on the battlements, the scene was familiar to me. I thought for a moment that it was déjà vu, then I realized it really had happened. The first time I visited the castle I saw you standing in almost the same spot. You won't remember, but you looked at me, and—'

'As a matter of fact I remember very well.'

'You do?'

'I also remember that you appeared to be shy. You looked away, then turned to go back to your car.'

'I was the only visitor still there and I thought maybe I should have already left.'

'So you ran, without looking back.'

'No. When I reached the gateway I *did* look back, but you'd gone.'

'I was hurrying down the tower steps. I wanted to talk to you, to stop you leaving.' He sighed. 'But I was too late…'

She had stopped in her tracks and was gazing at him, wide-eyed.

'Then when I saw you again at Arthur Jenkins's retirement party—'

'But surely you didn't recognize me after all those years, when you'd caught only one brief glimpse of me?'

'As a matter of fact I'd never forgotten you, and I knew you almost at once.'

'Is that why you gave me the job?'

'Partly,' he admitted.

'You never mentioned we'd seen each other before.'

'I wondered if you might remember.'

'I did… Sort of… I felt as if I knew you, but I didn't know why. I wondered if I might have seen your photograph somewhere…'

Then wonderingly, 'It's all so strange.'

'The Turkish and Arabic people call it kismet.'

'That's exactly what it feels like,' she said, and leaned against him contentedly, her head fitting snugly beneath his chin.

He kissed her hair, breathing in the fragrance of it, and feeling as though his heart were too big to fit into its allotted space.

Then, not wanting to appear soft, he returned to the practical. 'How is the ankle today?'

Straightening up, she smiled at him. 'Almost as good as new. The spray you put on seems to have worked wonders.'

'I'm pleased about that. Though I admit I was quite looking forward to carrying you again.'

With a seductive glance from beneath long lashes, she told him demurely, 'I dare say I'll need some help by tonight…'

He laughed joyously.

'In the meantime,' she added prosaically, 'when I looked in the kitchen, whatever you'd been cooking smelled delicious.'

'Hungry?'

'Ravenous.'

An arm around her slender waist, he commented, 'Unromantic but reassuring. Let's go and eat. Then when we've finished breakfast, if you think your ankle will stand it I'll take you up on the battlements.'

'I'm sure it will,' she said happily.

After a tasty breakfast at the kitchen table, Michael fetched their outdoor things.

'I know you're eager to do this,' he said as he helped her on with her coat, 'but promise you'll tell me if your ankle starts to hurt.'

Feeling cherished and cared for, she gave her promise, and they climbed the steps of the north tower and emerged onto the battlements.

The air was clear and fresh and the pale sunshine held more than a hint of warmth as, hand in hand, they walked slowly round the battlements. The views over the gleaming silver sea, the mainland coast, and the sweep of pale sand either side of the causeway were serene and beautiful.

Looking over the island's fertile countryside, she could see a collage of green fields and hills dotted with the orangey-yellow of gorse, and an occasional farmhouse, and on the seaward side the deserted beaches and rocky coves she and Michael had walked beside.

From the battlements, Slinterwood appeared to be quite close, and a little further on along the coast Jenny could see a farm and a hamlet of cottages, grey smoke rising from their tall chimneys and hovering, serene and orderly as a gathering of quakers.

After gazing at the picturesque scene for a while in appreciative silence, a catch in her voice, Jenny remarked, 'It must be wonderful to live here and to know all this beauty is yours.'

'I've always considered that in most respects I was a very lucky man,' Michael answered seriously. Then giving her a squeeze. 'And now I'm convinced that I'm the most fortunate man alive.'

That remark earned him a kiss, which he returned with interest.

After a while, becoming aware that her ankle was starting to throb, but reluctant to move, she shifted her weight onto her good foot.

Noticing that small movement, and appreciating the cause, he said firmly, 'We'd better be starting down. You can come up here as much as you like when your ankle is fully mended.'

Glowing at the thought, she allowed herself to be shepherded to the tower steps which, with his help, she managed to get down with comparative ease.

As they crossed the courtyard he glanced at his watch. 'I'd like to be back at Slinterwood before too long, so it might be a good idea for you to get straight into the car…?'

Wondering if he was planning to start work, she nodded, and allowed herself to be helped in.

'This way you can rest your ankle while I just make sure everything's safe. Mrs Blair will be over some time this afternoon to tidy up after us…'

When he came back he was carrying a large manilla envelope, which he tossed onto the back seat before sliding behind the wheel.

'All set?' he queried.

She nodded, and a moment later they were heading for the gatehouse.

It would have been a wrench leaving the castle had she been leaving for good. But the situation having altered so dramatically, and comparing how things were now to how they had seemed on her arrival at the castle yesterday, she left with a smile hanging on her lips.

The journey back to Slinterwood along the high coastal road was spectacular, and Jenny thoroughly enjoyed it.

Wondering what the actual distance was between the castle and Slinterwood, she remarked, 'It must be quite a long way for Mrs Blair to walk.'

'It would be by road, but when the weather's fine she takes a short cut.'

He pointed. 'See the stand of pine trees on the right? There's a path runs through them that leads first to the castle, and then down to the causeway.'

'What about when it's wet?'

'Oh, she doesn't walk then.' Michael grinned. 'She has a little car. She pops over to the mainland regularly to shop and play bingo.'

When they reached the house, once again it seemed to welcome her, and Jenny went inside as if she were coming home.

Everywhere was clean and tidy, and the fires had been lit, proving that Mrs Blair had been and gone.

As Michael helped her off with her coat Jenny said, 'Earlier you mentioned that you wanted to get back. Does that mean you're planning to start work?'

'No, not just yet. There's something I want to do first. Do you mind if I leave you for a short time?'

Though a little surprised, she answered, 'No, of course not.'

Settling her comfortably on the couch in front of the living-room fire, her shoes off and a selection of books by her side, he explained, 'I want to call on old Martha before lunch.'

At Jenny's questioning glance, he went on, 'Martha is well into her nineties. She used to work at the castle until my father died. Then she, along with her husband, Noah, and daughter, Hannah, finally decided to retire. Noah was almost a hundred years old when he died last year.'

'Does she live alone now?'

'No. After her husband's death, she went to live with her daughter... Now, you're quite sure you'll be all right?'

Touched by his concern, she answered, 'Quite sure.'

He stooped and kissed her lingeringly, as if he could hardly bear to leave her. Then, straightening, he headed for the door. His hand on the knob, he turned to smile at her and say, 'I won't be long.'

A few moments later she heard his car door slam, the engine start, and the car draw away.

For a while Jenny sat thinking over all that had happened while they had been at the castle, and marvelling at the way fate worked.

Yesterday morning she had been determined to leave both Michael and the island. But now, only twenty-four hours later, she was deliriously happy at the prospect of staying.

Though it was only a short time since they'd met, it was as if she had known and cared for him all her life. The thought was like a flare going up, making clear feelings she hadn't yet faced, and could hardly credit. How could she possibly love a man she had only just met?

Yet she did.

One day, if she was very fortunate, he might come to feel the same way about her, but at the moment all that really mattered was that he had no intention of going back to his ex-wife, that it was *her* he wanted with him.

Things had happened so quickly between them, and even

though no word of commitment had been spoken, and no promises made, she was content.

Although she wanted his love more than anything in the world, at the moment it was enough that he was tender and caring.

She was still savouring that newly found contentment when she heard the sound of the car returning and pulling up outside.

A minute or so later, to her surprise, there were voices in the hall, then the living-room door opened and Michael appeared, an old lady on one arm, and the manilla envelope he'd left in the car tucked under the other.

'Jenny, I'd like you to meet Martha… Martha, this is Jenny Mansell.'

Jenny swung her feet to the floor, but Michael said quickly, 'No, don't get up. Stay where you are. I've told Martha about your sprained ankle.'

Remaining seated, Jenny said with a smile, 'It's nice to meet you, Martha.'

As Martha gave a respectful nod Michael added, 'Martha has been with the family all her life.'

The old lady was tall and spare and dressed in black from head to toe. She wore long jet earrings and her pure white hair was in a neat bun. Though her face was as wrinkled as a walnut, her dark eyes were bright and alert, and she appeared to still have her own teeth.

When Michael had helped her off with her coat and she was settled in a chair by the fire, he suggested, 'What about a spot of brandy to keep out the cold?'

Then with a grin, 'And don't try to tell me I'm leading you astray, because Hannah mentioned that you always have a drop of "medicine" before lunch, to settle your stomach.'

Martha gave a cackle of laughter. 'And so I do.'

When Michael had supplied the old lady with a generous measure of cognac, he went to sit on the settee beside Jenny and explained, 'There's something I'd like you to hear, and, though Martha doesn't get out much these days, she offered to come and tell you first hand.'

As Jenny looked at him, puzzled and expectant, he took her hand and, twisting the heavy gold ring on her finger, went on, 'I'll start from when I first noticed the seal on your signet ring and recognized it as part of the old family crest. It was then I began to get an inkling of what might have happened.

'This morning, before I went up on the battlements, I had a quick look in the castle archives for some photographs I could vaguely recall seeing, and these are what I found. Martha recognized them both immediately.'

Reaching for the manilla envelope that he'd dropped on the coffee table, he opened it and passed her an old-fashioned, unframed, sepia photograph.

She found herself staring at a studio portrait of a young man sitting rather self-consciously beside a potted palm, his hands spread on his thighs.

Michael.

Only of course it couldn't be Michael.

Though the lean, strong face, the handsome eyes, and the well-shaped head of thick dark hair were identical, the moustache and the high, winged collar looked as if they belonged in the nineteen-twenties.

'Who is it?' she asked.

'My great-grandfather, Michael. I was named after him. Now take a good look at his right hand. See the signet ring on his little finger? Well, with a magnifying glass I was able to make out that the seal is a phoenix.'

Jenny was still puzzling over it when he handed her another photograph. Sitting in the same chair, by the same potted palm, was a young woman with dark eyes and dark hair, wearing a high-necked blouse and a long string of pearls.

Herself.

But again it couldn't be.

So who was it?

Almost immediately light dawned.

Watching her expressive face, he said, 'You've guessed it. Your great-grandmother, Jenny. The photographs must have been taken before she and Michael got engaged.'

'Engaged! So it was your great-grandfather who was the love of her life…'

Swallowing past the lump in her throat, she asked, 'What makes you think the photographs were taken before they got engaged?'

'Because he was still wearing the signet ring. When she agreed to marry him, he gave *her* the ring. However, before they could make any kind of formal announcement, he went down with flu. It turned to pneumonia, and within three days he was dead.

'As you know, he was a widower with a young son. He had married his own cousin when they were both very young, and after a brief and not particularly happy marriage his wife died in childbirth.

'When Michael became ill so suddenly and unexpectedly, his parents were away. They'd taken the child to Scotland to visit his maternal grandparents, and when they were summoned back it was to find that their only son was dead.

'Perhaps you can't blame them for being insular in their grief, but Jenny, who was heartbroken, found herself shut out, almost ignored.

'The only person who was sorry for her, and went out of her way to be kind to her, was Martha, who at that time was a young maid, about the same age as Jenny herself.

'Utterly devastated, as soon as Michael had been interred in the family vault your great-grandmother left, apparently for good.

'Martha told me all this before we set off for Slinterwood.'

There was silence for a time, then Jenny said slowly, 'I've often wondered if Gran had any connection with the island, and why I always felt it drew me. And now I know everything—'

'Not quite everything.'

She looked at him, her beautiful brown eyes fixed on his face.

'Remember the first time you came to Slinterwood, how familiar it was?'

'Yes,' she breathed.

'Well, of course your great-grandmother knew it well, and had Michael lived to marry her she would have gone there as a bride…'

'You're not saying her spirit…?'

He shook his head. 'No. Something altogether more mundane. But Martha will tell you the rest.'

While Michael replenished the old lady's glass, Martha took up the tale. 'One day, when you were a small child and living with your great-grandmother, she took you with her when she went shopping in Kelsay. After the shopping was finished, she put it in her car and took you into The Tudor Rose café, to buy you some lunch.'

The old lady's voice was a little croaky, as if she wasn't used to speaking so much these days.

She took a sip of her cognac before going on, 'Quite by chance, I was there with my daughter, Hannah. Though quite a lot of years had passed, your great-grandmother hadn't changed all that much, and she and I recognized one another, and got talking.

'While we chatted, your great-grandmother happened to mention that it had been her dream to see Mirren and Slinterwood again before she died.

'As luck would have it, the family were away, Slinterwood was standing empty, and Hannah and I were looking after things.

'So I suggested to your great-grandmother that she should

follow us back across the causeway, and take this chance to see both the castle and the house. She was only too delighted, and when we took her into the castle just briefly, and then over to Slinterwood, you came as well. You couldn't have been more than about three and a half, but you were a beautiful, intelligent little girl, who took notice of everything.

'I remember you were fascinated by the castle, and you loved Slinterwood. One thing that particularly took your fancy was the old pump in the larder, so Hannah primed it and pumped it to show you how it worked...'

Jenny smiled mistily. 'Though I've no recollection of actually going, that's obviously why everything was so familiar to me, why the house seemed to welcome me back...'

Getting to her feet, she went over to the old lady and, taking her hand, said sincerely, 'Thank you for coming specially to tell me. And thank you for being kind to Gran when she needed a friend. I was very fond of her.'

'Bless you, but you don't need to thank me,' Martha said. 'Your great-grandmother was a very nice lady. I only wish the young master had lived to marry her.

'Well, I'd best be getting back, otherwise I'll be catching it off Hannah for keeping lunch waiting.'

'We mustn't have that.' Michael rose and helped her into her coat.

Then, having put more logs on the fire, he turned to Jenny, and said, 'I'll be back as soon as I've seen Martha safely home. In the meantime I suggest you stretch out on the settee and put your feet up.'

As the pair reached the door Martha turned and said, 'You're very much like your great-grandmother, but I feel in my bones that you'll be a great deal luckier in love than she was.'

With that pronouncement, the old lady allowed herself to be escorted out.

The fire was blazing cheerfully, and, leaning back against

the cushions, Jenny put her feet up as she had been bidden, and sighed contentedly.

It had been a strange and eventful morning, but it couldn't have been a more wonderful one, she decided as she went over in her mind all that Michael and the old lady had told her.

Now she knew why the ring had meant so much to her great-grandmother, and why the island had always seemed to draw her...

Perhaps her destiny lay here with Michael. Perhaps they had been fated to meet, fated to carry on the love story that their great-grandparents had begun... Sighing, she stretched like a sleek and contented cat. She had never in her wildest dreams imagined being this happy...

Her thoughts grew scrappy as the warmth of the fire made her feel soporific, and, cocooned in a golden haze of euphoria, her eyelids drooped and she drifted into a doze...

CHAPTER TEN

JENNY awoke with a start to find she wasn't alone in the room. A woman was standing looking at her, a woman with blonde hair and blue eyes, wearing sheer silk stockings and a designer suit.

Jenny knew that face. She had seen it on the covers of glossy magazines.

But it couldn't be, she thought in confusion. Claire was in London.

Still her eyes continued to confirm what her brain was refusing to take in, that, far from being in London, Claire was right here.

And looking startlingly beautiful.

Jenny stared at her numbly, conscious of only one thing: Michael had lied to her. He'd told her that the relationship was over, but Claire's presence at Slinterwood went to prove the opposite.

'Who are you?' the newcomer asked sharply. 'What are you doing here?'

Pride insisting that she mustn't give herself away, Jenny found her voice and managed, 'I'm Mr Denver's new PA.'

'Then why are you lying down?'

'I've twisted my ankle, and Mr Denver told me to rest it.'

Clearly dismissing Jenny as any kind of competition, Claire relaxed and said, 'Oh, I see. What a nuisance for you.'

She sounded quite human. Almost pleasant.

As Jenny sat up and swung her feet to the floor, Claire queried, 'Incidentally, where *is* Michael? He doesn't seem to be around.'

'He's taking Martha home.'

The blonde grimaced. 'Any idea when he'll be back?'

'He said he wouldn't be very long.'

'He will be if Hannah gets talking to him. That woman could talk the hind leg off a donkey.'

'If he knows you're coming—'

'He doesn't know. I just made up my mind to come on the spur of the moment. It never occurred to me that he might not be here.'

Dropping into one of the armchairs, she put her handbag down, crossed her shapely legs, and, her voice not unfriendly, went on, 'I've an overnight bag with me if I don't manage to catch the tide, but I was hoping to be back in London by tonight.'

Then, her tone confiding, 'To tell you the truth, island life bores the hell out of me. Though I may need to be here a lot more after Michael and I are married again. Still,' she added reflectively, 'it should be worth it.'

Feeling hollow inside, Jenny made no comment, and after a moment or two Claire asked, 'How long have you been on the island?'

'Just over a week.'

'Do *you* find it boring?'

'No.'

'So how is the new book going?'

'It's beginning to take shape.'

'But he's not settled down to any actual writing?'

'No.'

'That's good. He hates to be disturbed once he's started. Has he taken you to see the castle yet?'

'Yes. We went yesterday.' To Jenny's eternal credit, her voice was steady.

'A cold, draughty hole, isn't it?'

'I thought it was beautiful,' Jenny said quietly.

'Oh, well, everyone to their taste.'

Then, discarding the jacket of her elegant suit, 'I stopped on the way for an early lunch, but I didn't have a drink so I'm *gasping* for a cup of tea.'

Heading for the kitchen, she added over her shoulder, 'Want one?'

Jenny shook her head. 'No, thank you.'

As the door closed behind the other woman, in a mad scramble to get away, Jenny pulled on her shoes, found her shoulder bag and mac, and, her only thought to escape before Michael came back, let herself out.

A red sports car was standing outside.

Following a sudden impulse, she tried the door.

It opened.

However, her hopes of using it to escape were dashed when the ignition keys proved to be missing.

Recalling the handbag Claire had left by the chair, she hesitated.

But going back into the house was too much of a risk. Michael might turn up at any moment and try to stop her leaving.

Paying no heed to her ankle, she hurried up the drive and along the road, glancing anxiously behind her from time to time.

When she reached the little copse that Michael had pointed out that morning, she veered off the road and took the cross-country path.

Only when she was hidden amongst the trees did she start to feel somewhat safer.

Where the sun hadn't penetrated, everywhere was still dripping, and the ground, thickly carpeted with brown pine needles, was wet and spongy beneath her feet and littered with storm debris, which made it slow going.

Her earlier numbness was still with her, the pain of Michael's treachery yet to come. As if she were slowly bleeding to death inside, all she could feel was a strange weakness, a lethargy. She longed to lie down on the saturated ground and find the blessed oblivion of sleep.

But she couldn't sleep until she was safely across the causeway.

Put to the test by the unstable ground, her ankle was throbbing badly now, but she almost welcomed the pain as an antidote to that terrible numbness.

After what seemed an age, she reached a point where a path went off to the right, and, looking through the trees, she could see the bulk of the castle on its rocky promontory.

Ahead she could make out the crescent of sea divided by the causeway, while in the far distance the mainland basked in the pale sunshine.

It looked a long way, and she admitted to herself that starting out on foot had been madness.

But she had had no choice.

Coming across a fallen tree, she sat down for a moment or two to rest her ankle.

Even that proved to be a mistake.

As though she had lost the will to battle further, she was overcome by a leaden sense of hopelessness and despair.

Only the thought of possibly having to face Michael again provided the necessary stimulus to bring her to her feet, settle her bag on her shoulder, and make herself go on.

She was descending the gentle slope that ran down to the road and the causeway when, on her right, a red sports car came into view.

Claire. The other woman was clearly on her way back to London.

Raising her hand, Jenny waved frantically, and, ignoring the pain, began to run. She had only gone a short distance when her ankle gave way and she went sprawling on the wet, uneven ground.

As she struggled to her feet the car flashed past, the driver looking straight ahead. By the time she'd picked up her bag and hobbled to the road, the vehicle was the size of a red toy car in the distance.

But that disappointment was almost instantly superseded by an even worse realization.

The tide was coming in. And fast. The sandy areas were almost covered. But she couldn't turn back now.

Picking up a length of old broken branch to use as a stick, she covered the last few hundred yards in record time.

Once she had set foot on the causeway, clearing her mind of everything but the necessity to get over as quickly as possible, she made what speed she could.

In what seemed to be an impossibly short space of time the tide, which had been rising stealthily, was starting to lap at the raised edges of the causeway.

She was still only about halfway across when the water began to swirl and eddy over the surface of the road, washing around her feet and wetting the bottoms of her trousers.

Looking at the far shore, she knew that at this rate she would be lucky to make it. But as both shores appeared to be almost equidistant, there was no point in turning back.

Her heart racing, she told herself firmly that she *had* to make it. There was no choice.

By the time she'd gone another couple of hundred yards, the water was starting to swirl around her ankles, dropping back a little between each assault, but returning with an inevitability that brought a surge of fear.

She tried to push herself into a splashing run, but at the added strain the stick proved to be brittle and snapped, making it too short to be of any use.

Dropping the useless piece into the swirling water, and

trying not to give way to the panic that filled her, she stumbled on as best she could.

When Michael returned to Slinterwood, his contented mood was blighted by the sight of Claire's sports car standing near the front door.

That she should come to Slinterwood at this time was the last thing he had wanted or expected.

Wondering just how long she had been here, and what she might have said to Jenny, he drew up alongside the red sports car, switched off his ignition, and jumped out.

The house seemed quiet and there was no sound of voices as he let himself into the hall. He hurried through to the living-room to find that the couch was empty and there was no sign of either of the women, but an expensive suit jacket was tossed over a chair.

He was about to go upstairs to look for Jenny when Claire came in from the kitchen carrying a round tray of tea. Putting it down on the low table, she said, 'So you're back.'

Without preamble, Michael demanded sharply, 'What are you doing here?'

'I wanted to talk to you.'

'I thought I'd made it clear that as far as I'm concerned there's nothing left to say.'

'Darling, don't be horrid.'

Ignoring that, he asked, 'Have you seen Jenny?'

'Your PA? She was here a little while ago. I asked her if she wanted some tea, but she said no thanks. I brought an extra cup in case she'd changed her mind.'

'So where is she?'

'How should I know? Probably in her room.'

'What exactly did you say to her?'

Frowning, Claire answered, 'Not a great deal. I asked her how the book was going, and if she'd been over to the castle.

'She said yes she had, and she thought it was beautiful.'

'What else?'

'Only that I wanted to talk to you.'

'Go on.'

'I told her that I wasn't planning to stay, and if possible I wanted to be back in London tonight.'

'And that's all?'

'That's all. Though I don't see why it matters.'

He was breathing a silent sigh of relief when she added, 'I might have been jealous, only she's so obviously not your type.'

Then coaxingly, 'Why don't you sit down and have some tea?'

'I'll dispense with the tea, thanks. I had a cup with Martha. So suppose you start talking.'

Reaching to fill one of the teacups, she said, 'I know the break-up was all my fault, but honestly I've learnt my lesson.'

When there was no response, she persevered. 'What we had at the beginning was really good, wasn't it?'

'But it only lasted until someone you fancied more came along.'

Sounding defensive, she said, 'I was bored out of my mind. You can't blame me for needing some fun while you were working…' Then, her tone softening, 'But you must know it was always you I loved, and still do.

'Give me another chance and I promise things will be different next time.'

He laid it on the line. 'I'm sorry, Claire, but there's going to be no "next time". Everything's over between us, and has been since I filed for divorce.'

'Don't say that,' she pleaded. 'I know you still love me and it's only your pride that won't let you admit it.'

'That's where you're mistaken. I *don't* still love you. When we were first married I thought I did, but what I felt for you soon died when I realized just what kind of woman you really were.'

'I can't deny I was unfaithful, but Jerry was very attractive, and because I was bored I let myself—'

'Don't take me for a fool.' Michael's curt voice cut across her words. 'I know quite well that Jerry wasn't the only one, that in the short space of time we were married you had a string of lovers.'

'None of whom meant anything to me.'

'Whether or not they meant anything to you is beside the point. I wanted a wife I could trust to keep her wedding vows. Not one that every time she was out of my sight I was forced to wonder whose bed she was in.'

'If I promise to change, won't you give me another chance?'

'It may sound trite, but leopards don't change their spots.'

'So this really is goodbye?'

'You'd better believe it.'

She sighed. 'Oh, well, I thought it was worth a try before I agreed to marry Marcus Conran.'

'Marcus Conran? By all accounts he's a lecherous old devil who's been married at least five times.'

'But he's stinking rich and quite besotted. And while the lump sum you settled on me was generous, it's dwindling fast, and a girl has to think about her future.'

With a glance at her watch she got to her feet, pulled on her jacket, and picked up her bag. 'I checked the tide-table, and if I get straight off I should just about make it.'

With a feeling of relief he showed her out.

As she got into her car her parting shot was, 'I won't invite you to the wedding.'

He watched the red car climb to the road and disappear in the direction of the causeway, before hurrying upstairs to look for Jenny.

Though all her things were still there, he could find no sign of her.

A hasty search proved she wasn't in the house, and the

shoes and mac she had been wearing were gone. Her injured ankle seemed to preclude the idea of a walk for pleasure, and the fact that her handbag too was missing told him the worst.

Badly shaken, he tried to tell himself that she wouldn't attempt to *walk* across the causeway. In her semi-crippled state, and with the tide on the turn, it would be utter madness.

But coming from the opposite direction, he'd seen no sign of her.

Hurrying out to the car, he wondered frantically just how long she'd been gone.

He didn't need to ask himself *why*.

His fingers fumbled when he tried to switch on the ignition, and, as though to underline his state of mind, he clashed the gears as he turned the car.

When he reached the road he put his foot down hard. With a bit of luck she wouldn't have reached the causeway yet.

As he flashed past the stand of pines, recalling that morning's conversation, he wondered if she had taken the cross-country route.

If she had, though the ground was uneven and the terrain rough in places, it was very much quicker than going by road.

He groaned.

Please God, let him be in time to stop her setting foot on that damned causeway.

During the brief time the castle had been open to the public, one couple had lingered too long and then attempted to drive through the rising water.

They had had to be rescued by boat—it had been summer and there had been plenty about—and their car retrieved at low tide the following day.

Then a walker trying to make a last-minute crossing had been swept away. Fortunately a strong swimmer, he had just managed to reach the shore.

The memory of those near tragedies pounding in his brain,

Michael rounded the bluff and took the serpentine road down the hill and past the castle at top speed.

Though the bends masked a great deal, there appeared to be no one on the road ahead.

Catching brief glimpses of the causeway, he could see that grey water was already swirling over it. He tried to tell himself that, surely, with an injured ankle, she wouldn't have attempted to cross.

Perhaps she was sitting down in the wood somewhere in too much pain to go on?

Well, if she was, at the very least she was safe, and if she hadn't strayed from the path he could find her quite quickly.

As he approached the start of the causeway, another possibility struck him: Claire might have picked her up. He would call Claire—hopefully she would stop long enough to answer it—and put his mind at rest.

Rounding the final bend, he brought the car to a skidding halt. He was pulling his mobile from his pocket when the sight of a figure some halfway across the causeway stopped his heart.

'Oh, dear God,' he breathed. Once the water was this deep, it came in with terrifying speed. If he took the car, even though it was a four-wheel drive and fairly high, it was doubtful whether he'd be able to get it back.

But even as the thought went through his head he knew he had no choice. He'd never be able to reach her in time on foot.

It might not even be possible by car.

Every nerve in his body tense, he drove down the incline and onto the causeway, his speed causing a wake of water on either side, and headed for that distant figure.

Her darkened gaze fixed on the far shore, which appeared, if anything, to be getting further away, Jenny battled on. But she knew herself to be going slower and slower.

The water was now almost calf-deep, and it was like trying

to wade through treacle. Her feet and legs were numb with cold, but even through the numbness each step was a small agony.

Though she felt dazed, incapable of coherent thought, a small part of her mind knew with dreadful clarity that she wasn't going to make it.

Then, through the blood pounding in her ears, she heard what sounded like a car engine and someone shouting, calling her name.

Knowing she must be hallucinating, she ignored it and kept on as best she could.

There was a splashing noise, as though someone was running, a hand seized her arm and swung her round and strong arms swept her up.

A moment later she was bundled unceremoniously into the front seat of Michael's four-wheel drive, water that had washed in over the sill when he'd opened the car door slopping round her feet.

His face pale and set, he slid behind the wheel, and without a word carefully and deftly turned the big car, and started back to the island, steering between the marker poles.

All his instincts screamed at him to hurry, but, knowing that if water got into the engine they would be finished, he engaged a low gear, and, keeping up the revs, crept forward through the rapidly rising water both as fast and as slowly as he dared.

It was touch and go, and when they reached the shore, hardly able to believe they'd made it to safety, he drove up the incline before stopping to fasten their seat belts.

Clenching her teeth to stop them chattering, Jenny managed hoarsely, 'Thank you… I wouldn't have made it if you hadn't—'

Turning on her, he demanded with a kind of raging calm, 'Have you no sense at all? What in heaven's name made you do such an idiotic thing?'

Though he didn't raise his voice, his white face and the

grimness of his mouth told her that he was absolutely *furious*.

'I—I'm sorry,' she stammered.

'And so you should be! Another minute or so and it would have been too late.'

Shrinking away, she bit her lip to hold back the weak tears that threatened. So she'd been stupid. But she was damned if she'd let him see her cry.

Without another word, he started the car, and they drove on in silence.

Shock had set in, adding to the cold and fatigue, and he could feel her shaking uncontrollably. A quick sideways glance showed him her eyes were closed and her face was ashen.

Seeing the unmistakable traces of tears on her cheeks, he berated himself for being such a brute to her. But he'd been so terribly afraid that he was going to lose her after all, and when he'd known for certain that she was safe all his previous fear had metamorphosed into anger.

By the time they reached Slinterwood, Jenny was barely conscious and only vaguely aware of being helped from the car and carried into the house and up the stairs.

He brought her night things from her room, and as gently as he could, stripped off her clothes, dried her wet feet and legs, helped her into her nightdress, and tucked her up in his bed.

Almost before her head touched the pillow, she was fast asleep.

As he stood looking down at her small face, with its black fans of lashes and pale lips, he thanked God that she was safe.

Now he'd found her again, it would have finished him to lose her.

Jenny awoke with a start and sat bolt upright with a little cry, her heart throwing itself against her ribcage like a crazy thing.

It took a second or two to realize she was safe in bed. Then, her panic subsiding, and reassured by the sight of the familiar room, with its shaded lamps and blazing log fire, she leaned weakly back against the pillows while her heartbeat returned to normal.

Though her ankle throbbed dully, physically she felt almost as good as new, whereas mentally, recalling how Michael had lied to her to get what he wanted, she felt churned up and desolate.

But, having been brushed by the wings of death, she knew she owed him a big debt of gratitude, even if the future did look bleak and empty.

Recalling how quietly furious he'd been, she wondered if he was still mad with her.

Anticipating some degree of relief that she was safe, she had been totally floored by his unexpected anger.

Now, thinking about it, she suddenly recalled an incident she had witnessed some years ago, but that had stuck in her mind.

A mother, holding a little boy by the hand, had been waiting at a busy crossing when a fellow pedestrian had spoken to her. Temporarily distracted, she had relaxed her hold, and the boy, seeing a friend on the opposite pavement, had pulled free and run into the road. Brakes squealing, the car had managed to stop with just inches to spare.

As the boy had begun to howl with fright, the mother had dragged him to safety. But instead of hugging and kissing him, as Jenny had expected, she had shouted at him and shaken him angrily, before bursting into tears of relief.

But surely that reaction would only happen if you loved the person involved, and Michael didn't love her, she thought bleakly. He loved Claire.

At that instant the door opened and Michael himself came in, carrying a large tray.

He was dressed in stone-coloured trousers and a fine polo-necked sweater in a dark green that picked up the colour of his eyes.

Her heart turned over at the sight of him, and she caught her underlip in her teeth and bit hard to hide the surge of emotion.

'So you're awake—that's good. I thought you should have some food inside you before settling down for the night.'

He both looked, and sounded, himself again.

Putting the tray on the table by the fire, he came over to the bed and, studying her closely, asked, 'How are you feeling now?'

'Fine, thank you,' she answered.

'Would you like to eat in bed or by the fire?'

Though she wasn't hungry, she answered without hesitation, 'By the fire.'

Then, deciding to take the bull by the horns, she added jerkily, 'And then I'd like to sleep in my own room, in my own bed. Alone.'

'Very well, if that's what you still want to do once we've had a chance to talk.'

What could he possibly say? she wondered dully. After Claire's visit, he couldn't very well deny he had lied about taking her back.

Turning down the bedclothes, he helped her out of bed and into her gown. Then, having carried her over to the fire, he settled her in one of the comfortable armchairs, and queried, 'Warm enough?'

'Oh, yes, thank you.'

Putting a napkin over her knee, he filled a plate with lamb casserole and handed it to her, before taking a seat opposite and serving himself.

The casserole, which proved to be good and tasty, was followed by fresh fruit and cheese.

In spite of her inward misery, once she had forced down the first mouthful she managed to eat a reasonable meal.

Though the air was thick with unspoken questions and re-criminations, they finished eating without a word being spoken.

Only when they reached the coffee stage did Michael break

the silence to ask a question he was sure he already knew the answer to. 'So why did you run away?'

'You know perfectly well!' she cried. 'You deceived me, told me a pack of lies, just to get me into bed again!'

'I did no such thing,' he said flatly. 'When I told you that Claire and I were finished—'

'You were lying!' she choked.

'I was *not* lying,' he denied quietly.

'But she *told* me that you and she were getting married again.'

'That was what she was *hoping,* but it was far from the truth.'

'Oh,' Jenny said in a small voice.

'When I told you the relationship was over, I meant every word. I had absolutely no intention of taking her back. As a matter of fact until I saw you again at Jenkins's retirement party I had no intention of *ever* remarrying.'

Jenny caught her breath, wondering if he could possibly mean what she thought he meant.

But, his voice level, he was going on, 'And Claire didn't really want *me* back. All she wanted was a secure meal ticket, and she saw me as a slightly better bet than the next candidate she has lined up.'

'The next candidate?'

'An old roué with five failed marriages behind him, a penchant for young, beautiful women, and unlimited millions to buy himself what he wants.'

'And you're not upset about it?'

'I might be if Claire was some innocent ingénue. But she isn't. Claire knows quite well what she's doing, and presumably she thinks it'll be worth it.'

Cynically, he added, 'So long as he keeps the cash supply flowing, and gives her plenty of freedom, it will probably work quite well until she becomes a rich widow.'

Still hardly able to believe it, Jenny persisted, 'You're not sorry it's finally over?'

He shook his head. 'Anything but. I've always believed that marriage vows should be meant and kept, and that children should be born into a home that was loving and stable. It would never have been that way with Claire.'

Jenny sighed. 'It's just that the ending of a relationship can be sad.'

'Personally I regard this as a happy ending.' He took her hand. 'Or, rather, the beginning of a new relationship. One that I hope and believe is destined to go on and last a lifetime and beyond.'

'You don't mean…' She stopped, afraid to put it into words.

'That's exactly what I mean!'

He lifted her hand to his lips and dropped a kiss in the palm, before going on, 'How could you think for one instant that after all we've shared I would take Claire back? It must have been obvious that I wanted you, needed you, so much that I couldn't think straight.

'It's been like that since the first moment I set eyes on you. All those years ago, when I saw you standing in the castle courtyard, you seemed achingly familiar, as if I'd always known you, as if I'd been waiting all my life for you.

'Then as I watched your car drive away that first time I felt empty, desolate, as though I was losing something that was infinitely precious. For months you haunted me. I saw your face in my dreams, and wakened with it still in my mind's eye. I found myself looking for you everywhere I went, in London's bustling shops and stores, on the busy pavements, in passing cars, the reflections in shop windows, and in the quiet park.

'For perhaps the first time I fully understood the meaning of the word *desideratum*—something desired as necessary. When I failed to find you, I felt an emptiness, a need, that took a long time to lessen. Seeing you again and getting to know you brought all those emotions back in force, and I feel more strongly than ever that we belong together.

'How do you feel?'

As those forest-green eyes looked into hers she said softly, 'The same.'

'That's good, because there's nothing we can do about it. It's destiny. You do believe in destiny?'

'Yes. I felt as if I was destined to come to the island, to the castle, and Slinterwood, as if I belonged here.'

'I'm quite certain you do. And I'm equally certain that it's our destiny to complete the love story our great-grandparents began. Though they weren't fated to be happy together, we'll make up for it.'

Lifting her, he settled her on his lap, and for a long time, his cheek against her hair, they sat in contented silence.

Eventually, when the fire began to die low, he said, 'Time for bed, don't you think?'

At her nod, he asked wickedly, 'Do you still want to sleep in your own bed, in your own room? Alone?'

'That depends.'

'On what?'

'On what inducements you can offer.'

'Well, let me see… I could…' Putting his lips close to her ear, he whispered erotic suggestions that made her toes curl and heat run through her.

Feigning indifference, she said, 'I suppose that *could* be worth staying for.'

'I'll make sure it is,' he promised.

Having set her carefully on her feet, and stripped off her night things and his own clothes, he carried her back to bed and got in beside her.

While his lips traced the pure line of her jaw and his hands started to caress her, she asked, 'Is your middle name really James?'

Stopped in his tracks by the unexpected question, he promised, 'You'll find out when we get married.'

'Are we getting married?'

'We're not only getting married, but in our very own chapel.'

'How wonderful…' Then dreamily, 'How many children would you like?'

Against her throat, he said, 'To begin with, I want you all to myself for a while, then perhaps we could start with a little girl just like you.'

'I was thinking of a couple of boys first… But perhaps it wouldn't be a bad idea for them to have an older sister. Then—'

A finger to her lips, he said, 'Whoa there!'

'You don't want a big family?'

'I'd love a big family.'

'That's good, because I—'

Stopping her lips once more, he said severely, 'But it may never happen if you don't stop talking and let me get some practice in.'

As she started to laugh, his heart swelling with love, he kissed her.

For a time the only sounds in the room were the rustle of logs settling in the grate and her little gasps and moans as, with hands and lips and tongue, he followed through with his whispered suggestions.

Both were conducive to practice.

Turn the page for an exclusive extract
from Harlequin Presents®
RAFFAELE: TAMING HIS TEMPESTUOUS VIRGIN
by
Sandra Marton

"IN THAT CASE," Don Cordiano said, "I give my daughter's hand to my faithful second in command, Antonio Giglio."

At last, the woman's head came up. "No," she whispered. "No," she said again, and the cry grew, gained strength, until she was shrieking it. "No! No! No!"

Rafe stared at her. No wonder she'd sounded familiar. Those wide, violet eyes. The small, straight nose. The sculpted cheekbones, the lush, rosy mouth...

"Wait a minute," Rafe said, "just wait one damned minute...."

Chiara swung toward him. The American knew. Not that it mattered. She was trapped. Trapped! Giglio was an enormous blob of flesh; he had wet-looking red lips and his face was always sweaty. But it was his eyes that made her shudder, and he had taken to watching her with a boldness that was terrifying. She had to do something....

Desperate, she wrenched her hand from her father's.

"I will tell you the truth, Papa. You cannot give me to Giglio. You see—you see, the American and I have already met."

"You're damned right we have," Rafe said furiously. "On the road coming here. Your daughter stepped out of the trees and—"

"I only meant to greet him. As a gesture of—of goodwill." She swallowed hard. Her eyes met Rafe's and a long-forgotten memory swept through him: being caught in a firefight in some miserable hellhole of a country when a terrified cat, eyes wild with fear, had suddenly, inexplicably run into the middle of it. "But—but he—he took advantage."

Rafe strode toward her. "Try telling your old man what really happened!"

"What *really* happened," she said in a shaky whisper, "is that…is that right there, in his car—right there, Papa, Signor Orsini tried to seduce me!"

Giglio cursed. Don Cordiano roared. Rafe would have said, "You're crazy, all of you," but Chiara Cordiano's dark lashes fluttered and she fainted, straight into his arms.

* * * * *

Be sure to look for
RAFFAELE: TAMING HIS TEMPESTUOUS VIRGIN
by Sandra Marton
available November 2009 from Harlequin Presents®!

Darkly handsome—proud and arrogant
The perfect Sicilian husbands!

RAFFAELE: TAMING HIS TEMPESTUOUS VIRGIN

by

Sandra Marton

The patriarch of a powerful Sicilian dynasty,
Cesare Orsini, has fallen ill, and he wants atonement
before he dies. One by one he sends for his sons—
he has a mission for each to help him clear his
conscience. But the tasks they undertake will
change their lives for ever!

Book #2869

Available November 2009

Pick up the next installment from Sandra Marton

DANTE: CLAIMING HIS SECRET LOVE-CHILD
December 2009

www.eHarlequin.com

HARLEQUIN *Presents*

kept for his *Pleasure*

She's his mistress on demand—but when he wants her body and soul, *he will be demanding a whole lot more! Dare we say it…even marriage!*

PLAYBOY BOSS, LIVE-IN MISTRESS
by Kelly Hunter

Playboy Alexander always gets what he wants… and he wants his personal assistant Sienna as his mistress! Forced into close confinement, Sienna realizes Alex isn't a man to take no for an answer.…

Book #2873
Available November 2009

Look for more of these hot stories throughout the year from Harlequin Presents!

www.eHarlequin.com

REQUEST YOUR FREE BOOKS!

 HARLEQUIN *Presents*

PASSION GUARANTEED SEDUCTION

2 FREE NOVELS PLUS 2 FREE GIFTS!

YES! Please send me 2 FREE Harlequin Presents® novels and my 2 FREE gifts (gifts are worth about $10). After receiving them, if I don't wish to receive any more books, I can return the shipping statement marked "cancel". If I don't cancel, I will receive 6 brand-new novels every month and be billed just $4.05 per book in the U.S. or $4.74 per book in Canada. That's a savings of close to 15% off the cover price! It's quite a bargain! Shipping and handling is just 50¢ per book*. I understand that accepting the 2 free books and gifts places me under no obligation to buy anything. I can always return a shipment and cancel at any time. Even if I never buy another book, the two free books and gifts are mine to keep forever.

106 HDN EYRQ 306 HDN EYR2

Name	(PLEASE PRINT)	
Address		Apt. #
City	State/Prov.	Zip/Postal Code

Signature (if under 18, a parent or guardian must sign)

Mail to the **Harlequin Reader Service:**
IN U.S.A.: P.O. Box 1867, Buffalo, NY 14240-1867
IN CANADA: P.O. Box 609, Fort Erie, Ontario L2A 5X3

Not valid to current subscribers of Harlequin Presents books.

Are you a current subscriber of Harlequin Presents books and want to receive the larger-print edition? Call 1-800-873-8635 today!

* Terms and prices subject to change without notice. Prices do not include applicable taxes. Sales tax applicable in N.Y. Canadian residents will be charged applicable provincial taxes and GST. Offer not valid in Quebec. This offer is limited to one order per household. All orders subject to approval. Credit or debit balances in a customer's account(s) may be offset by any other outstanding balance owed by or to the customer. Please allow 4 to 6 weeks for delivery. Offer available while quantities last.

Your Privacy: Harlequin Books is committed to protecting your privacy. Our Privacy Policy is available online at www.eHarlequin.com or upon request from the Reader Service. From time to time we make our lists of customers available to reputable third parties who may have a product or service of interest to you. If you would prefer we not share your name and address, please check here. ☐

HP09R

HARLEQUIN *Presents*

TWO CROWNS, TWO ISLANDS, ONE LEGACY

A royal family torn apart by pride and its lust for power, reunited by purity and passion

THE ROYAL HOUSE *of* KAREDES

Look for the next passionate adventure in
The Royal House of Karedes:

THE GREEK BILLIONAIRE'S INNOCENT PRINCESS
by Chantelle Shaw, November 2009

THE FUTURE KING'S LOVE-CHILD
by Melanie Milburne, December 2009

RUTHLESS BOSS, ROYAL MISTRESS
by Natalie Anderson, January 2010

THE DESERT KING'S HOUSEKEEPER BRIDE
by Carol Marinelli, February 2010

www.eHarlequin.com

HP12467

I ♥

HARLEQUIN *Presents*

BROUGHT TO YOU BY FANS OF
HARLEQUIN PRESENTS.

We are its editors and authors
and biggest fans—and we'd
love to hear from YOU!

Subscribe today to our online blog at
www.iheartpresents.com